Praise for Angels Unaware

"Gifted new author Lisa DeAngelis captivates with a highly unusual tale. Her distinct voice has inviting powers reminiscent of Carson McCullers in *The Heart Is A Lonely Hunter* and Harper Lee in *To Kill A Mockingbird.*"

- Brent Monahan, author of *The Bell Witch/An American Horror Story* and *The Jekyll Island Club*

"Lisa DeAngelis infuses a poor mining town in the thirties into the very wallpaper of this story of Darcy Willickers as she recants the intricacies of her life in a lyrical voice showing the strength that only the downtrodden can muster. Recommended."

- Hope Clark, author of *The Carolina Slade Mysteries* and *The Edisto Island Mysteries*

"A treat from beginning to end. Lisa DeAngelis has created unforgettable characters and a story that grips you from the first page. I was drawn into the world of the Hospitality Inn. Darcy and Luca were so vivid, they almost jumped off the page. I highly recommend this book. You can't put it down."

- John McDonnell, author of *The Playwright's Bridge*

"Lisa DeAngelis has composed a real page-turner. The story draws you in and doesn't let go."

- Mark Allen, Times Publishing Newspapers, Inc.

"This tale rolls fast and furious off the tongue of Darcy Willickers, flavored with sauce and cynicism. Imagine Cinderella smashing the glass slipper and telling Prince Charming to go pound sand and you'll appreciate a character too grounded in depression-era realities to ever see herself as a victim."

- Dave Roth, author of *The Femme Fatale Hypothesis*

Angels Unaware

Lisa DeAngelis

Regal House Publishing

Published by
Regal House Publishing, LLC
Raleigh, NC 27612

ISBN -13 (paperback): 9781646030699
ISBN -13 (epub): 9781646030941
Library of Congress Control Number: 2020941111

Interior and cover design by Lafayette & Greene
lafayetteandgreene.com
Cover images © by Ure/Shutterstock

Regal House Publishing, LLC
https://regalhousepublishing.com

Printed in the United States of America

for my husband, Al,
and for my children Kate, Luke, and Lily

"Be not forgetful to entertain strangers for thereby some have entertained angels unawares."

– Heb. 13:2

1

Bitter Fruit

It was to be a strange life, though we didn't know it then, and rich in a poor way, and sadder than we could have imagined, and happier than we would have dreamed. And I guess you could say that of every life, but we didn't know it then. There was a lot we didn't know then. Do we ever know what it is that we're about, and when we do, is it ever in time to change anything? Too late. Deep, black words, these are. Deep as the quarry where we swam one summer and black as the water in it. A child drowned there once. His body never surfaced, and since nothing starts a legend faster than a missing body, some mystical-minded locals began saying that he'd dived so deep that he'd stumbled upon a secret place of such exquisite beauty and peace that he hadn't wanted to come back to Galen anymore and would remain in his watery world forever.

The truth is: The child drowned. I told Luca the story one day while we were in the quarry, and he looked so serious that I dove under the water and held my breath as long as I could, and when I came up again, I arranged my face in a ghostly way and tried to scare him. He wasn't really scared, but all the same, he got out of that black water and told me he didn't like being where somebody had died. I said that I bet there wasn't a square foot of ground anywhere on earth where somebody hadn't died sometime. It never occurred to me until years later that the quarry would have been a better place to hide Jesse than the orchard where the dog kept trying to dig him up.

If Jewel were alive, she'd say, "Oh, shut up, Darcy, can't we talk about something besides dead people?" And she would remind me that the dead boy had drowned a good thirty years before I was even born, and to stop telling it like I'd got the information firsthand.

Memory can be a funny thing. Past and present entwine like a braid of human hair, until you can't be sure what happened thirty years ago and what happened yesterday, what you knew and what you only heard about. And sometimes, without trying, you can even remember something that hasn't happened yet. It was like that with us. One day, while I was sitting out on the front porch, as the sun was going down, I remembered that I would love him. If only I'd remembered sooner. But as it was, I wasn't any better than the blind woman who had passed through Galen once. She had the gift and could tell you what color the next man who walked down the road would be wearing, or what you'd wind up eating for dinner on the third Tuesday of next month, but nobody was much interested in what they'd be eating, and the blind woman never could prophesy anything more important than dinners and an occasional lunch.

What I mean is that all the things that really matter are mixed in with the things that don't matter at all, and you can drive yourself mad trying to tell the difference. Jewel knew a man once who'd done just that. His wife had just had a baby and left him with his father while she went out. The father got the idea of going in the house to get some chewing tobacco, and he left the baby in the hammock in the yard. When he came back, he found the baby crushed to death under the bough of a fallen tree. Twenty years later, he was still telling whoever would listen that he'd only left the baby for a minute, just a minute and not a second more. The point is that being crushed to death is an important thing, and chewing tobacco isn't, but there they were side by side. Anyway, they finally had to get some men from the madhouse to come and take him. Even in the asylum, he kept telling his story over and over again, but at least in there, he found new people who hadn't heard it before and showed more interest than us here in Galen.That's why I always tried not to think about things too much. The madhouse is full of thinkers, whose eyes went bad squinting, trying to read more into their lives than ever was there.

But sometimes, summoned or unbidden, images come to you and catch you unawares, snatches of things that used to be and aren't anymore; one such for me was a July day when I watched him chopping wood in the heat, his tanned skin taut over muscle, shining with sweat, and I could hardly look at him for fear of giving myself away. Other times, I can feel him on top of me, the sweet heaviness of him; and I can smell him, his skin scented with woodsmoke and heather. Or it's his voice I hear, a velvet voice like the dress that Jewel used to wear on Christmas day. She gave me a puzzle one Christmas with a thousand pieces to it, and no picture on the cover to show what it was supposed to come out to be. "You'll figure it out," she told me, but she was wrong.

If Jewel was here with me now, she'd say, "When you can't figure a thing out, go back to your earliest memory of it. What was the first thought you can remember thinking? For heaven's sake, think, Darcy, think…."

My earliest observation about Galen Creek, Pennsylvania, was that there wasn't much to live for there, at least not much that you could tell right off. The women in Galen were mostly mothers, and the men were mostly miners. Mothers and miners, except for a few who farmed for a living. They shared something more than bitterness and something less than sympathy. They weren't often kind to each other, and certainly never to us. But in Galen, no one expected kindness. Things were too hard for that, or maybe not hard enough. Everybody watched over their own miserable little lives and left everybody else to do the same.

Jewel thought them poor in spirit and said that was why they couldn't be kind to anyone but their own. It was being kind to people who you didn't even know that counted most. Jewel said a lot of things that didn't mean much, and only a fool would have listened too closely.

Jewel was born someplace in Texas to the Reverend Roy

Willickers and his wife, which probably accounts for her early distrust of men of the cloth. She had an angelic face and a shapely body, and boys tended to sniff around her worse than dogs. At sixteen, she was so popular that when she got pregnant, she couldn't be sure just who of the three boys had made her that way. Honest to a fault, she told them so. Her candor took all the romance out of the situation, and nobody was too interested in marrying her after that.

The Reverend Willickers soon got wind of her predicament and he took her to a woman who gave abortions. But Jewel, unimpressed with the woman's filthy back room, soured on the idea. Besides, she liked babies and wasn't averse to having one. Her father, enraged by her refusal, beat her black and blue. So that night, she left Texas for good. Or at least that's how Jewel told it. You couldn't always believe her, not because she lied, but because she often embellished or omitted details so as to make the story move faster and be more interesting. In fact, the only thing she ever found intolerable in another human being was their inclination to tell too long of a story.

Jewel was vague about how she'd ended up in Galen, and I wonder sometimes if she really knew. She claimed that she had just been "following destiny." Jewel was fond of words like *destiny*. She liked telling fortunes with picture cards and told everybody more about their futures than they ever wanted to know, but she was never as accurate as the blind lady who foretold dinners.

I was born in a hotel, just off the turnpike, and Jewel named me Darcy after her mother who'd died young. Jewel hadn't any money to pay for her room, but the hotel clerk, seeing how pregnant she was, let her stay the night anyway. He even found a midwife to help her. That was the night, Jewel said, that persuaded her to go into the hospitality profession, on account of that clerk's kindness to a stranger.

A week later, Jewel was arrested for vagrancy and me along with her. Anybody else might have seen that turn of events as a major setback. But Jewel said her arrest turned out to be the best thing that ever happened to her. The police brought her up before the justice of the peace, who took one look at her and fell desperately in love. He not only kept Jewel out of jail, but he brought her home with him to his house in Galen Creek. The justice was an old man, but Jewel wasn't one to hold age, sex, or even species against a person. She liked men, women, children, and animals with as much discrimination as a whore has for sailors. The old man was a widower who'd never had any children, and he doted on Jewel as both the wife he'd lost and the child he'd never had. When he died a year later, he left her a goodly sum of money and his ramshackle old house, so that she might turn it into an inn and fulfill her dream of joining the ranks of innkeepers of America.

I was barely a year old when the old coot went and not one for talking. If I could've talked, I'd have told Jewel then and there to be frugal with the justice's money. As it was, by the time I was six or seven and old enough to advise, she had gone through half of it in frivolous ways. Her most ridiculous extravagance, and the one that never failed to make me mad, was the massive sign she had printed that hung on the side of the dilapidated house, placing a heavy burden on the shingles. It read: The Hospitality Inn. And underneath, it had a slot for a smaller sign to read either: Vacancy or No Vacancy. In all the years I would live at the inn, we never once were able to show the No Vacancy sign.

I was three when Jewel got her first boarder, Duncan—an art student on summer break from college. He'd discovered Galen while searching the countryside for landscapes to paint. Later I found out he came from rich people who lived in Philadelphia, and he proclaimed both Jewel and the inn to be "delightfully quaint." That was my second observation about life. Rich people always find poverty picturesque. Duncan's summer break turned into a two-year "hiatus" to learn about "the quintessence of life." I don't remember Duncan very well, but I think he must have been an idiot. It was said I bit him once. How else was I to demonstrate my feelings toward guests? This formed the foundation for my lifelong attitude to innkeeping in general and the Hospitality Inn in particular. I hated the loss of privacy, the constant wearying need to make pleasant conversation, maintaining the pretense of caring about the minutiae of other people's lives.

When I was four, Caroline was born, and I found myself saddled with a sister I welcomed as much as smallpox. Caroline had Duncan's blue eyes and black hair, and she was the most beautiful baby anyone had ever seen, just as she would grow into the most beautiful girl the residents of Galen had ever seen. Jewel's second baby by Duncan was comparatively plain, but Jolene would grow up to be a genius, so it didn't matter so much.

After Jolene was born, Duncan decided he'd had about enough of our quaintness, and that life in Galen wasn't any more meaningful than life in Philadelphia, so he went back to his family and his money. Poor Jewel, ever the good sport, kissed him goodbye and wished him well.

"How could you let him get away like that?" I demanded later when I was old enough to demand. Missed opportunities always made me cross.

"What else could I have done?" she answered nonchalantly. "He wanted to go."

"Dammit all! You could have made him pay for the trouble he caused you, not to mention two years' room and board." It still gnawed at me twenty years later that that little Philadelphia turd had ate and drank and slept and got his pole greased for a whole two years free of charge.

"Oh, Darcy," Jewel exclaimed, waving me away. "What're you so mad about? The man gave me happy times and two beautiful daughters. Why, I'm the richer for having known him."

I never understood Jewel. Sometimes I even wondered if she was my real mother or if roving gypsies had left me to her when they broke camp. I looked nothing like her, and everything she did, or failed to do, made no sense to me. Her name for instance. Once, while rooting in the attic, I came across a birth certificate for Margaret Mary Willickers, and another document that legally changed her name to Jewel Willickers. I could understand her dislike for her first name, but why keep Willickers, which was just as silly as Margaret Mary. There were no answers to questions like that. It could only be chalked up to Jewel being Jewel.

My mother could remember in detail events of ten years ago, but completely forget what had happened the day before. And she could not seem to recall that which I most wished to know—the identity of my father.

"One of those boys must have looked more like me than the others," I persisted.

"No," she mused. "I can't say as they did. And they didn't have your mean streak either. No, not one of them. What's so important about fathers anyway? The reverend was the only sour note in my otherwise sweet existence. You should be glad you don't have to be bothered with one." (Jewel always referred to Willickers as "the reverend," and never as her father.)

Perhaps it was that Caroline and Jolene had the same father, while mine was not only different but unknown, that divided us from the very beginning. That, and my need to be obeyed and respected. Even as a child, I refused to play games with my sisters. Less than four years seperated us, and I figured they wouldn't respect me if I indulged in childish games, so I hung back, aloof, and watched a little contemptuously, just to show I was a cut above. My strategy worked because they always paid attention when I told them to come into the house or to do their chores. Jewel said I was born with a natural gift for intimidation, and it was certainly true enough with my sisters. But there were people in Galen who were a lot harder to scare off.

Just about everybody in the town believed that Jewel was a whore, which struck me as funny since after the art student, Jewel had sworn off men for good. She still liked them all right, and she had no regrets, but men made more problems than solutions as far as she was concerned, and she didn't want any more problems than she already had. I guess people thought she was a hussy just because she looked like one. She had wild hair that was always messed up, no matter how many times you combed it, and made her look as if she'd just gotten out of bed. And she had a tart's way of walking, with her pelvis out and her hips swaying. Galen had a whorehouse, but it was out in the middle of the woods and the girls pretty much kept indoors, so I'd never seen one close up, and couldn't say for sure how they walked. Or maybe, it was the railroad men who came to the inn for dinner, often staying overnight, that convinced the people of Galen of wrongdoing in the Willickers's household.

Jewel liked the railroad men; she liked their inclination to enjoy the moment that maybe was the result of constant sojourning, and their ready acceptance of whosesoever's company they found themselves in. I liked the railroad men because they were good for business. At ten, I'd decided that it would be best if we didn't rely solely upon the justice's money, and I made up my mind that the inn would be a profit-making venture. The trouble was that Galen wasn't exactly known for its tourism. In fact, even if people had heard about us, it was unlikely they'd ever find the inn on their own. That's where the railroad men were useful. They met weary travelers every day and had the opportunity to direct them wherever they wanted. After we started regularly having them for dinner, the railroad men began sending people to us. Though we never filled our rooms to capacity, the finances improved a little.

Matters would have improved still further if Jewel and I could have agreed on a management policy. Our typical guest consisted of some vagrant who had little or no money to pay for lodgings, and had, by some process that would forever remain a mystery to me, found his way to our door. Clearly, the poorest of persons possessed an incredible sense of direction because no rich man ever managed to include the inn on his travel agenda, not after Duncan anyway. Mostly, we accommodated men without jobs, pregnant girls without husbands, and dogs and cats whose ribs showed beneath mangy fur. That was how we came to get Old Sam. I was thirteen when Jolene brought him home, a flea-ridden bag of bones, ugly as sin, and with a big appetite. I was all for pushing him out the door and telling him to get, but they all whined and pleaded (Jewel the loudest) until I gave in. Of course, bathing the mutt fell to me. Jewel and my sisters were afraid his ticks would give them fever; and when the dog ate a rabbit the following day, and threw up his meal all over the carpet, I cleaned it up. Jewel and the girls protested that dog vomit was entirely too disgusting to deal with so soon after breakfast.

As much work and bother as Old Sam turned out to be, I preferred him over the two-legged guests who came through our doors. I'd curse and spit as Jewel led our penniless guests through the lobby with the full measure of her grace and charm, just as if they were millionaires. I'd mutter loudly that we barely had enough food to feed ourselves, in the hope they'd overhear and be shamed into leaving. But Jewel would just shush me, telling our visitors that I was bad-tempered, and they mustn't take it to heart.

As I've said, but it bears repeating, I hated the hospitality profession with a passion and wished with all my heart and soul that a tornado would come and blow the inn right off the map. But it never happened. Every morning when I woke up, the decrepit building stood as it had the night before, demanding an endless number of increasingly wearisome tasks. On winter mornings, I'd get up early to bring coal up from the cellar to keep the stoves going, careful not to smother the embers. If the fire went out, I would have to start over, and the coal took forever to take the flame. I'd stand in the icy kitchen, freezing and cursing and wishing I'd catch pneumonia and die and be put out of my misery. Jolene was too little to do chores, and Caroline was of little help on account of her being prone to coughs and colds. Once the coal had caught, I'd start kneading the dough for breakfast bread. Jewel had a morbid fear of lighting ovens, ever since she'd singed her eyebrows trying to light a cigarette from one in fifth grade. She wasn't one for chores either but preferred to descend the stairs just as coffee was being served and ask everyone if they had slept well. The hostess act—that, she did real well. After breakfast, there were dishes to be washed, rooms to be cleaned, wood to be carried, and always, always in winter, more coal to be shoveled in, so that—God forbid!—the fire didn't die and I'd have to start all over again.

After my morning tasks, I sometimes went to school, when I felt I could not escape the duty. I liked to read—Jewel had given me the complete works of Shakespeare one Christmas—and I never had time to read in school, what with the teacher always talking and distracting me. I didn't much care for my classmates, and they didn't like me any better—perhaps because when I turned fourteen, my hair started to go gray. Kids whispered stories of graveyard curses, witch's spells, and other nonsense. Many an eye was blackened for making fun of me or Jewel, and I was feared, if not liked.

When Caroline and Jolene started school, they fared better. Beauty covers a multitude of sins, and Caroline was so pretty that people were willing to forgive her for having Jewel for a mother and me for a sister. And Jolene had a winning way about her and could make people laugh, so they forgave her too. I always made sure that Caroline and Jolene attended school regular. I intended that they should both go to college someday, and as for me, when everybody was settled and everything was taken care of, then I'd leave Galen and live a fascinating life far, far away.

Jewel often talked to me as if we were the same age—perhaps due to my lack of friends, and the secret we later shared. In mind, heart, and soul, I felt much older than my mother. I suppose that experience embitters some and educates others, but Jewel remained undaunted by life's challenges; inside, she remained the naïve, innocent Margaret Mary Willickers, sixteen years old and fresh from Texas.

Once I asked her why she hadn't married the justice of the peace.

"Because his name was Elwood," she replied.

"Well, if that isn't the stupidest reason I ever heard!" I exclaimed impatiently. "You could've married him and called him anything you liked."

"No. No matter what I called him, Darcy, I'd still be thinking Elwood up here," she proclaimed gravely, tapping her head.

I wondered sometimes if she'd ever had "anything up there." She had made up her mind against marrying Duncan—even if he'd had the notion of asking her—because she'd come upon him tweezing his nose hairs in the bathroom mirror. It proved to be an image she couldn't shake, Jewel declared. No romance, she told me, could endure scrutiny. She seldom spoke in this manner to Caroline or Jolene, even when they were old enough to hear it. She was afraid to make them cynical, she confided. Even then, she knew it was too late for me.

For all our differences, Jewel and I got along harmoniously enough, except when it came to the justice's money. She was forever thinking up ways to spend it, and I was forever thinking up new ways to hide it. Finally, I suggested we save it for Jolene and Caroline's college fund. If my sisters stayed in Galen after graduation, I told Jewel, they'd surely end up mothers married to miners, and Jewel—who was never able to settle upon anything for more than an hour or two, though she was always most sincere at the time—agreed. Then, however, we were free to argue about how to raise money going forward. My brilliant idea came to me one night as I lay in bed, just on the verge of sleep. I sat bolt upright, leapt from the bed, flung open the door, and raced down the hallway to Jewel's room.

"I've had a brilliant idea," I told her excitedly. "We'll take the train to Philadelphia and find Duncan." At her perplexed expression, I reminded her. "The art student, remember? The father of your children? We'll remind him of his responsibilities and, in exchange for a cash settlement, we'll promise to keep quiet about his two illegitimate children."

"That's blackmail, Darcy," she said reprovingly.

"No, Jewel, that's raising funds."

"I would never, never, never in a million years—"

"Why the hell not?"

"It's immoral, that's why."

This, from a woman who'd born three illegitimate daughters. I went back to my room in a snit.

We might have made a go of the inn if only we'd had more than one bathroom. But for another toilet, my life might have turned out completely different. As it was, we had just the one, and when the toilet got stopped up, and my plunging was of no use, we'd have to use the outhouse. The North Pole could scarcely be any colder than that outhouse on a February morning, when piss froze before it hit the bottom.

If the one bathroom wasn't problem enough, our lobby was dull and old and faded. The draperies were thin, the rugs were threadbare, and the sofa's springs were sprung. Even the bell on the front desk failed to chime. Besides that, the roof leaked in spots, dripping brown water into metal buckets when it rained. Floors had rotted out in patches. Once Mr. Lillicrap fell from the second floor—the one Jewel liked to call "the mezzanine"—clear down to the lobby and busted his leg. Good thing he had no money to pay his bill in the first place, or he might've sued us.

Lillicrap had his peculiarities, but he was by no means our most peculiar guest. That contest would have been too close to call. He was an old gentleman who owned one double-breasted white suit of which he was very proud. He wore it every day winter and summer, and it was always cleaned and pressed. Doubtless he must have cared for it in his room every night as if it were a firstborn son. It was a formal kind of suit, though he never went anywhere more formal than the whorehouse in the woods, and I don't believe dressing up was required, since their clients were mostly miners. Lillicrap was a drunk, and even though he owned a white suit, and his speech never slurred, and his gait never staggered, he was a drunk just the same. We could always tell when he was drunk because he would take his pillow off his bed and sleep in the claw-foot bathtub. Jewel never cared much one way or the other where the guests slept, until one night when Miss Mahoney, a spinster with skin as white as her hair and razor-thin fuchsia-painted lips, went to use the toilet. She had just arranged herself on the seat when Mr. Lillicrap came out of his stupor. I'd never heard a woman scream so loud or so long. Miss Mahoney woke up all the other guests in clear defiance of the signs I'd tacked up in the hallway requesting absolute quiet after nine o'clock.

My sympathies were entirely with Mr. Lillicrap, who was even more startled than Miss Mahoney, having taken the old maid for a ghostly apparition. After that night, I wanted them both evicted but Jewel wouldn't let me.

"I'm surprised you don't want to wait for a blizzard so you can throw them out in the snow, Darcy," she said. Evicting anybody, Jewel felt, would be tantamount to tampering with the workings of fate, and if there was one thing she would never do above all others, it was tamper with the workings of fate. There was no getting around it. Jewel was simply not cut out to be a landlord, and I would have to think of other ways to make money.

It was then that I had the idea of taking in wash. "Nobody in Galen has money to throw away on having their laundry done!" Jewel protested, with a laugh. But I was thinking of cities and towns beyond our provincial little Galen. It seemed I was the only one in my family who realized that Galen didn't reach to all horizons. I certainly never forgot it, and often, it was all that kept me going.

In Parkville—the next town after Galen—people were a little better off, and I was determined to convince all those high-class hicks that they couldn't do without my service. I went door to door, explaining that I was with the Willickers Laundry Association, located in the heart of Galen, Pennsylvania, in the business district. For a meager sum that would scarcely be missed from the household budget, they could say goodbye to chapped, red hands forever. My pitch would hardly have clinched the deal, but there was, I knew, nobody in the world more competitive and jealous of little things than a Parkville housewife. And I had had the foresight to wait for the mailman and commit to memory the names of women up and down the lane. And so it was that on my first call, when Mrs. Johnson attempted to close the door in my face, I managed to slip in that her neighbor across the way, Mrs. Kelly, had purchased my services because she thought washing clothes too menial and low class for words. Naturally, after that, Mrs. Johnson had to give me all her dirty clothes rather than admit to herself that she wasn't as worthy of the luxury as Mrs. Kelly.

Thereafter, every Monday, I would pedal my bicycle, with a succession of six wagons tied to the back, up and over the hill to Parkville, where I would pick up dirty laundry. The inn had an old washing machine with two rollers that wrung water from the clothes. Jewel helped for the first week, but it quickly became clear that she had little tolerance for other people's dirty underwear. Two of my clients were new mothers, which meant mounds of dirty diapers, the washing of which convinced me at fourteen never to have children, and just to be on the safe side, never to have a husband either.

Before long, Jewel found her own way of making money. She hung out a hand-printed sign that read: Sister Jewel, Mystic Reader and Advisor. The paint on the sign was still wet when Reverend Hamilton had her arrested for fortune-telling. Reverends had a way of popping up in Jewel's life and ruining things. Having stayed overnight in jail before, Jewel wasn't too put out. The sheriff let her out the next day with a warning.

Two weeks later, I caught four of my fingers in the wringer of the washing machine, breaking them and putting an end to the Willickers Laundry Association.

That was a tough winter. Jewel and the girls caught the grippe, and I had to nurse them with one bandaged hand. Jewel insisted on smoking her Camels and filling the sick room with smoke. Then, she'd cough her brains out, and I'd have to run out for whiskey and lemon. We'd have been able to renovate the whole inn and travel round the world just on what Jewel could have saved on Camels. But as soon as her cough had calmed a little, she'd light one up again, claiming that tobacco would surely kill the infection. As for me, I never got sick. Whoever my father was, he must have been hardy if not good-looking, because an illness never arrived that could lay me low. Not that I would have minded coming down with something so that I, for once, could be the patient instead of the nurse.

While Jewel was sick in bed, she found an advertisement in a magazine for mail-order astrology books. She ordered and read a number of them, and then she hung out a new sign: Jewel Willickers, Astrological Consultant. When the reverend sent the police to arrest her, Jewel claimed that astrology was a science just like any other. It said so in the books she'd read. But they took her away just the same, and I had to pay a large part of the money I'd saved doing laundry to get her out.

Having to give up the money I'd worked so hard to obtain—and for which I had broken four fingers!—left me with a burning hatred for the reverend. I've put off telling about Reverend Hamilton because I hate the thought of him, but I suppose I've got to confess it all sooner or later.

The reverend and his wife had lived in Galen their entire lives. In fact, they were good friends with the justice, that is until Jewel came to live with the old man. At first the arrangement seemed to suit everything just fine. The reverend and his wife, Gale, used to visit with Jewel and the justice and play a friendly game of cards or two. You might expect Reverend Hamilton to be horrified at the notion of a young girl and an old man living together out of wedlock, but you'd be wrong. The reverend knew which side his bread was buttered on. The justice put a lot of money in the collection box every Sunday and even paid for the pews, so the reverend was reluctant to offend him.

The strain on their friendship began when the justice told the reverend that he was intending to leave his house to Jewel after his death instead of the church. But the straw that broke the camel's back was the night Reverend Hamilton tried to kiss Jewel and she slapped his face. Hamilton wasn't bad looking, if you didn't mind the persnickety type. Unfortunately, Jewel couldn't stand the persnickety type, and she told the justice of his friend's advances. The two men came to blows, and Hamilton was humiliated in front of his own wife when the justice, a man twice his age, kicked the daylights out of him.

After that, Reverend Hamilton and his wife never spoke to the justice and Jewel again, and when the justice died, Hamilton spitefully refused him burial in the small graveyard beside the church. But Jewel said that one bit of dirt was just as good as any other, and she had his body taken over to the cemetery in Parkville, where she visited him every year on his birthday. She even made me and the girls come with her to sing "Happy Birthday," complete with candles and cake, which we ate by the graveside wearing party hats.

Jewel never said anything, but I knew she was a little afraid of the reverend, not for herself, but for us. She predicted that when he got tired of tormenting her, he would turn his attention to Jolene, Caroline, and me, thinking us easier targets. As we got older, I saw that she was right.

One Monday morning, in fifth grade, I found myself the target of twenty sneering classmates. They called Jewel names and made fun of my hand-me-down clothes. Then Maryann Gates declared that me and my family weren't Christians, and we were going to burn in hell because the Reverend Hamilton had told them so. In fact, he'd devoted all of the previous day's sermon to our family of blasphemers and heretics.

Tough as I was, I was still only eleven, and a little put off at finding the odds so grievously stacked against me. I hoped Miss Blount would come to my defence, but she just looked at me doubtfully and clucked her tongue. For lack of a better idea, I spat at Maryann and landed a wad of spittle right on her forehead, (I was a regular marksman with saliva) which got me into trouble with Jewel who said spitting was a low thing to do.

After school the next day, Miss Blount asked me to stay and have chocolate milk with her.

"Would you like a cookie to go with that milk, Darcy?" she asked.

"Sure," I replied.

From her bottom drawer, where she kept her "cough medicine," she withdrew a paper sack and took out a wafer.

"You must be wondering why I asked you to stay."

"Not especially, Miss Blount."

"No?"

"No. I figure you'll get around to telling in your own time. Besides, I got nothing to do till five o'clock. Then I got to get home and start supper."

"You cook supper in your house?"

I nodded and burped. The cookie was stale. Probably Miss Blount had been saving that cookie for years, just waiting for some dumb little child she could bribe.

"Can't your mother cook, Darcy?"

"Sure she can," I said.

Miss Blount sighed, looking at me with elaborate patience, as she often did with her dullest students. "Then why doesn't she?"

"Because she's afraid of ovens," I answered honestly. In those days, I still had some candor left, just enough to get me in trouble.

"Afraid?" She peered over her glasses. "Afraid of what? An oven can't chase you all over the kitchen," she remarked with a laugh.

Miss Blount was making Jewel sound foolish, and I didn't like anyone doing that but me. "She isn't afraid of it chasing her around the kitchen," I said patiently, as if Miss Blount, too, might be one of those dull students. "She's afraid of lighting it and catching fire and being burned to death. Jewel had a dream once where she saw the inn in flames."

"You call your mother Jewel?"

"That's her name."

Miss Blount shook her head. "This is all very disturbing, very disturbing. How can a grown woman be afraid of a simple thing like lighting an oven?"

"Everybody is afraid of something," I said defensively.

"Look at how you screamed and jumped around and made a fool of yourself when a little field mouse came into your classroom. With you, it's mice. With Jewel, it's ovens. If you think about it, Miss Blount, her fear makes a lot more sense than yours. I mean people get burned to death all the time, but nobody's ever been devoured by a field mouse."

I was enjoying her blushing and stammering, but it was over all too quickly. "And what are *you* afraid of, Darcy?" she asked, changing the subject.

"Nothing."

"Nothing at all?" She raised her skinny, penciled-on eyebrows.

"Well, nothing like mice or ovens. My fears aren't simple-minded like that."

I saw her eye twitch at being called simpleminded, but she persisted, nonetheless. "Then what, Darcy?"

I was too young to understand that my brains were being picked for evidence, so I answered truthfully, "Sometimes, I'm afraid I'll never get out of Galen, that I'll grow old and die here." For truly, at that time, I could not have imagined a worse fate for myself.

"And what makes you want to leave so badly? Do you hate it so?"

"No, not especially. But there are places, Miss Blount, so many places and cities and towns beyond Galen."

"What kind of places do you mean, Darcy?"

"Places like—well, like Kathmandu." I was too excited now to be careful.

Miss Blount wriggled her nose as if she suddenly smelled something sharp and sour. "Kathmandu?" she asked. "Whatever is that?"

"It's the capital of Nepal," I told her.

"Where is that?"

"I don't know exactly, but it's very far from here and I like the way it sounds. Kat-man-du," I proclaimed, rolling the syllables around on my tongue.

The teacher frowned. I had managed to sidetrack her and

she was annoyed. "But what about the inn, Darcy? Are things hard for you at home?"

"No. I eat regular, and I've got my own room." Having your own room was no small distinction in Galen, where most kids slept with no less than three siblings to a bed. I was mighty proud of my independence, but Miss Blount was not impressed.

"There are more important things than rooms and food, Darcy," she said firmly.

"Like what?" I asked, unable to imagine what could possibly be more important than eating regular.

"Well, religious convictions, for one. Christian ideals…"

That did it. As soon as she said the word *Christian*, her ploy was laid bare.

"What has your mother done about your religious upbringing?" she asked over her glasses. "We never see you in church."

I didn't answer immediately. The closest Jewel had ever come to religious instruction was when, on a real nice day and the weather was fine, she'd throw her arms wide and say, "On a day like this, can't you just feel God with both hands?" Jewel was no churchgoer, partly, I think, due to her conviction that Reverend Hamilton would have had her stoned at the altar. With me and the girls, however, she neither told us to go to church, nor to stay away.

"We're not Protestant," I finally blurted out in our defense.

"Then what are you?"

"I don't exactly know the name of it. It—it's Jewel's religion!"

"You mean to tell me that your mother has her own religion?"

"Kind of."

"And where is her church?" Miss Blount asked disapprovingly.

"The inn, I guess."

Miss Blount pursed her lips. "I can tell from our talk today, Darcy, that your mother hasn't done right by you or your sisters."

"Miss Blount, you're wrong. Jewel's always done right by us. No mother ever did better."

"All children think that, Darcy," she said, almost kindly. "Nevertheless, I feel that it is my duty to report the neglect of your religious training and suggest that Reverend Hamilton find good Christian homes where you girls can receive proper instruction. Of course, we'll try to keep you three girls together, but—"

I was so mad by then that I didn't hear the rest. That afternoon, I experienced my first cold rage. Before, I'd only had hot rages, the kind where your cheeks turn red and you feel like you've suddenly got a fever. That time, in Miss Blount's classroom, was different. I moved not a muscle in my face; it was as if someone had covered me with a snow cold blanket, and with the cold came the calm, the calm that could be so frightening to those who later saw it in me.

"Miss Blount."

"What is it, Darcy?"

I leveled my eyes to meet hers and saw her shift in her chair. "I want you to know that I could never let anybody separate my family. It may not seem like much of a family to you, but it's mine, and I will always keep it together…no matter what I have to do, or who I have to hurt."

She looked away, suddenly uncomfortable. "You're too young to know what's best for yourself and your sisters."

I kept my eyes locked on her own. "We belong together, Miss Blount, and there's nothing I won't do to keep us together. And if anyone ever tried to divide us, I'd do anything to stop them, even things so terrible that a good Christian lady like yourself couldn't even begin to imagine them."

She stared at me, mouth dropped open in surprise, and I thought I saw her shiver. She shuffled some papers before saying, "My, my, my, it's getting on to five o'clock, and you did say you had to be home by then."

I was almost amused, watching my teacher's desire to save me wrestle with her greater desire to save herself. And, of course, with someone like Miss Blount, the latter always won out, and I never heard talk about taking us away from Jewel again. Which was as it should be. Sometimes the family you find yourself in, though not the one you might have chosen, is the family you belong in for reasons that are beyond knowing but become important later in life. I know that's convoluted, but it's the best I can explain it.

Reverend Hamilton was another story. He'd had Jewel arrested four times for fortune-telling. Jewel kept changing her title, hoping to get him off her back. Sometimes she used the picture cards to tell the future, sometimes a crystal ball, or tea leaves, or plain old playing cards. She called herself by turns, advisor, reader, sister, mystic, seer, and spiritualist. But it was all "evil divination" to the reverend and the police, and she got locked up just the same. But never for very long, so that it was more a nuisance than anything else.

I know now what made the reverend so dangerous. He could do things that were wicked and hateful and convince himself that he was doing right, so that the more wicked he got, the more righteous he got, too, and the more elevated he supposed himself to be.

Sometimes, you remember things more clearly than you experience them and understand more about an event the farther away you get from it. Looking back, I think that Hamilton loved Jewel almost as much as he hated her, but he didn't love her or hate her for herself, but for the parts of his own self he saw in her. Or maybe, he hated himself for loving a woman like Jewel, when his own Good Wife Gale left him unmoved.

I'll say one thing: If Gale Hamilton had believed herself any more good and chaste and pure than she already did, she'd have built a shrine to her own likeness and worshipped at the altar. One year, around Christmas time, the church put on a play about the night Jesus Christ was born. Naturally, Gale, being the minister's wife, got to run the whole thing, including picking out the six- to ten-year-olds in her Sunday school who would play the parts. Predictably, Joseph, the innkeeper, and the Three Wise Men were chosen from the biggest church-supporting families in Galen. But didn't everybody get a surprise when none other than Herself came riding in as Mary on a cardboard donkey. I guess when it came right down to it, Gale couldn't bear for anyone else to play the role that was clearly written for her. She looked positively murderous when little Jamie Baumeister couldn't remember his line and answered yes, when asked if there was any room at the inn. Perhaps Gale would have preferred to play the role of Jesus Christ, a part that was given to the only one on stage who didn't overact, a plaster of Paris dummy. Had it been possible, I swear Gale Hamilton would have wrapped herself in swaddling clothes and jammed herself in that manger.

Gale Hamilton should never have been a mother, or the reverend, a father. It didn't seem right that a person had to get a license to hunt or fish, but anybody, no matter how godawful or crazy, could have children. Jewel might not have been everybody's first choice, but when I considered the Hamilton boys, I always felt myself real fortunate.

Maybe it was because of Reverend Hamilton's constant pressure to be so good—or at least to appear so—that Aaron and Seth turned out so bad. There's some kind of scientific law that if a thing's pushed too far one way, it'll eventually swing back the other way, with all the more force for having been pushed.

Aaron Hamilton was a little older than Caroline, and his brother, Seth, was born the same year as Jolene. Their house was just a mile down the road from the inn, but their father had issued strict orders that they were never to play with us, which probably made the prospect all the more tempting.

As I said before, even as a child, I did not play, preferring to keep my dignity and authority intact. Seth was content to fool around with Jolene and Caroline, but Aaron was forever begging me to join in with their games. When I steadfastly refused, he'd sit out the game with me and try to make conversation.

I never liked Aaron Hamilton and instinctively tried to avoid him. Even young as he was, there was something unnatural about him. Jewel realized it, too, after the funeral parlor incident. Most people in Galen held funerals in their own homes and thought that those who availed themselves of funeral parlors for this purpose demonstrated a lack of respect for the dead. Jewel worked briefly for a funeral director fixing dead people's hair. She often said that dead people made the best customers because they never complained. (Of course, on the other hand, she said, they never tipped either.) Sometimes, when the reverend was called on to comfort the bereaved, he'd bring his boys with him. Once, Jewel left a body to get a comb from upstairs; when she came back down, she found Aaron doing something terrible with the body. She never would say what he was doing exactly, just that we were to stay away from the Hamilton boys and to promise that when she died we'd lay her out at home and bury her near the inn. And not to worry about her hair. She said once she was dead, she didn't much care how her hair looked.

I tried to avoid both boys, but Aaron was not to be discouraged, despite my ignoring him and yelling at him to leave me alone. Aaron always came back for more abuse, and eventually I came to understand why.

One afternoon, while the girls and Seth were playing hide and seek and Aaron was leaning back against a tree, watching me read, the reverend appeared. Usually he was too busy off ministering to poor unfortunates to keep track of what his boys were up to. But that day, furious that his sons had defied his orders never to play with us, he made Aaron take his shirt off and hug an apple tree. Then he made a cat 'o-nine-tails and whipped Aaron until great red welts rose on his bare back. Then he did the same to Seth, who screamed each time the whip cut him, though he dared not run. But Aaron never made a sound. That was the difference between them. Somewhere inside Aaron Hamilton was a scream, and many years would pass before Galen heard it.

Next day, both boys were back, and curiosity made me break my silence. "After the beating you took yesterday," I said, "how can you take the chance coming back here?"

Suddenly, Aaron looked very serious without his usual smirk. "Nothing will keep me away from you, Darcy," he said gravely. "Not flood. Not pestilence. Not famine. Not hell nor high water. Nothing." And the way he said it made me shudder. This was not the idle pledge of a smitten school boy but the first stirrings of obsession, an omen of things to come. The oak is always in the acorn.

To say I became childhood friends with Aaron would be exaggerating, but sometimes he wore me down to the point where I would answer him when he asked me something, if all it took was a yes or no, and I might listen halfheartedly when he talked. The year I turned thirteen, Aaron started confessing things to me, telling me things I'd have slept better not knowing.

"Know that fire in old man Zook's barn?" he asked, grinning.

I nodded yes. Old man Zook was a Mennonite with queer ways and Aaron for some reason had always hated him.

"I did it," he said proudly. "Whooosh, that barn went up like human hair."

A few minutes passed before I gathered myself enough to say, "Why?"

He shrugged his thin shoulders. "I love watching fires. They're so pretty. All orange and gold."

"Two of his horses got killed," I said dully, feeling sick to my stomach. "And the old man nearly got killed himself trying to free them."

"Ain't my fault," he said, and I didn't argue with him.

Seth was almost as bad as his brother, but stupidity and clumsiness kept him from being as dangerous. Lacking Aaron's cunning and imagination, Seth would willingly tag along with his brother's schemes.

I never told Jewel about what Aaron had said about old man Zook's barn. She'd have called the sheriff and he wouldn't have believed me; even if he had, there was no proof, and Jewel would likely bring trouble down on our heads once again. So I kept my mouth shut and watched the old man painstakingly rebuild his barn with arthritic hands and a gimp leg. I never heard him complain. I guess he was used to having the things he worked for destroyed and resigned to the tedious labor of trying to restore them. Sometimes, my conscience bothered me, but I had my own family to think about. If I had helped old man Zook, then it might be our inn that Aaron took a match to next.

Most people in Galen would have liked nothing better than to see the Hospitality Inn go up in flames. There's no denying the place was an eyesore. Years of neglect had taken their toll, and the sorry state of the guests we attracted didn't help matters any.

Jewel was prone to romanticizing innkeeping, but for me, there was nothing romantic about having a hoard of strangers regularly tramping through your house. "But we meet such nice people," she'd insist. As for me, I lived in fear that one night one of those nice people would slit our throats for cigarette money while we slept. I bolted my door every night, though Jewel and the girls refused to do the same. Jewel thought the best way to protect yourself from something was never to think about it, to never even consider the possibility. Whereas I was certain that the best form of self-protection consisted of imagining every dark thing of which humanity was capable and putting a sturdy barrier between yourself and it.

I never forgot any of the guests who passed through over the years, which isn't to say I remembered them either. Instead, they floated in some kind of limbo in the back of my mind, and from time to time, one or the other would step forward.

When Norma and Leon came to mind, I always had to laugh. They'd discovered the inn on their way to find factory jobs in Pittsburgh. One day, a pounding came at the door that was so powerful and immediate it rattled the hinges and shook the casing. I opened the door to find Leon on the stoop

"Open then the door," he proclaimed grandly. "You know how little while we have to stay, and, once departed, may return no more." As it happened, they stayed for a year. They were strange people, or I should say, strange for the world, but ordinary for the Hospitality Inn. Of course, they didn't have enough money to pay, so Jewel told them about the inn's special savings program, that only she herself had ever heard of before. Norma and Leon had the distinction of being the only couple whose failure to pay didn't bother me. I figured that what they provided in entertainment more than made up for what they lacked in cash.

Norma was fat and fortyish, but she had a pretty face which is what everyone always says about fat girls, but she really did. Leon was thin and had a homely face and a querulous disposition, not unlike my own. Naturally, I liked him immediately. There were enough bones of contention between them to keep a dog chewing for years, and we all wondered how they had ever gotten together in the first place.

Norma hated Leon's mother, and though she hadn't seen the woman in more than three years, just knowing that she continued to draw breath was enough to vex Norma. "Go to your mother, Leon!" she'd say. "She's waiting for you with open legs—I mean arms." Then he'd go for her throat and Jewel would step between them.

Leon complained that Norma never kept up with her wifely chores, and it was her neglect of the laundry and ironing that particularly annoyed him. In spite of their limited funds, Leon was quite the dandy when it came to dress. "I never got no clean socks," he lamented. So one day, when Norma had had enough of his sock talk, she marched upstairs, filled the bathtub, threw in Leon's dirty socks, sprinkled them with powdered soap, removed them dripping wet, and flung them over the banister, where they landed across his upturned face. "Here's your socks," she announced, "clean as a whistle."

For Leon's part, his major crime in his wife's eyes was the gold front tooth he proudly displayed when he smiled. Norma was convinced he had chosen gold over porcelain just to spite her by making himself look like a farmer. Most people harbor no ill will against farmers. Some are even grateful to them for feeding humanity. Norma was not one of these. But as with all our likes and dislikes, loves and hates, there was a reason for it.

Norma had grown up on a farm in Kansas where her father used to wake her at five each morning to feed the chickens. It had gotten so that Norma not only hated her father and chickens, but farms and farmers, and feathers and dirt, and anything that could even remotely remind her of the whole experience. When she came of age, she fled to New York City where she met Leon, as far from being a farmer as she could imagine. He'd been selling insurance at the time and always wore nice clothes, with his hair neatly slicked back with pomade. "Now here we are, twenty years on, and the bastard's gone and gotten himself a gold tooth and started parting his hair down the middle just to drive me insane!" she cried.

They quarreled about Leon's drinking, or as Leon preferred to call it, his "love of the grape." Leon made his own wine and brandy and drank it faster than he could make it. And when in his cups, he would recite verse at length; we girls were an appreciative audience to his recitations, but Norma would just roll her eyes and call him Count Shit-in-the-Sink.

The worldly hope men set their hearts upon turns ashes—or it prospers; and anon, like snow upon the desert's dusty face lighting a little hour or two—is gone. This he read from a book he frequently kept under his arm like ministers did the bible.

When I asked his advice about how to become a successful innkeeper, he told me: *Into this universe, and why not knowing, nor whence, like water willy-nilly flowing: and out of it, as wind along the waste, I know not whither, willy-nilly blowing*, which wasn't really helpful.

A year after their arrival, I had to ask them to leave. I hated to see them go. But their fights had reached a pitch where Mrs. Hennessy, across the way, was calling the sheriff several times a week, and my aversion to the police was greater than my liking for Leon and Norma.

On the day they left, Leon drew me aside. "I don't have no money to pay you, Darcy," he told me regretfully, "and I'm the sorrier for it. But there are three things I am gonna leave you that are better than money. One is the truck."

Leon had patiently taught me how to drive the rusted-out heap that he and Norma had arrived in. Grateful, I nonetheless wondered if his leaving it had anything to do with the fact that he'd been unable to get it started for the past month.

"The other thing I'm leaving you is this." He picked up his shotgun, the one I'd always been afraid he'd one day use on Norma.

"What're you leaving that for?" I asked dubiously.

"Oh, you'll understand what to do with it when the time comes."

"How will I understand?"

He spread his arms wide and looked up at the sky and I knew I was in for another recitation.

Then to the rolling heaven itself I cried, asking, 'What lamp had destiny to guide her little children stumbling in the dark?' 'A blind understanding!' heaven replied.

"Here," he added, handing me a leatherbound tome. "Everyone should have a book of Persian poetry."

RUBAIYAT OF OMAR KHAYYAM was etched in gild leaf across the tattered cover.

"Who's Omar Khayyam?"

"Some smart old Persian guy."

After a while, he turned back to me and said, "You know, when I was a young man living in New York City, I used to love to go to the theater. And it seems to me when you think about it long enough, we're all just actors in one another's plays. We each have our part to perform, whether we want to or not. Maybe your part in my play was to help me and Norma out while we was down on our luck. And maybe my part in your play is to give you this gun. I got a feeling someday you'll have a use for it."

2

A Checkerboard of Nights and Days

In those days, my only ambition, modest as it may seem, was to avert disaster, and being in the hospitality profession made this pretty hard. Inviting strangers into your house is a surefire way to leave yourself wide open to the ever-present dangers that lurk all around just out of sight. I can't remember a time when I wasn't convinced that one of those strangers who mysteriously divined their way to our door would be our undoing, and for years, I waited, without realizing I waited, looking down the road that led up to the inn, waiting for the one to come who would change things forever. Yet strange enough, when he came that summer, the fourteenth summer of my life, he passed unrecognized.

I never liked Jesse James, but I certainly never feared him. He seemed too ridiculous a person to fear. Take his name. I didn't need anybody to tell me that Jesse James wasn't his real name. (Later, I would discover that his real name was Wistar Paist.) He roared into our lives on a motorcycle, disturbing the dust in the road, wearing a black helmet and a black leather coat. To me, he was comical. Younger than Jewel, with dirty blond hair and opaque gray eyes, he stood not more than five and a half feet tall, with a build so slight and wiry, and a chest so slender and narrow it was almost concave. And he called himself Jesse James! I couldn't wait till Jewel heard that one. She always laughed at people who put on airs, and I was betting she'd wet her pants when she got a look at Mr. James, so it came as a real surprise when she didn't think he was funny at all. Looking back, I suppose it was their shared adventures in nomenclature that kept her from appreciating the humor of such a skinny little guy taking the name of a famous outlaw. I guess Margaret Mary Willickers wasn't about to call the kettle black.

Anyhow, they hit it off right away, and so discreet was Jewel that it took a full week for me to realize they were sleeping together. Oh, they were subtle all right. Going to bed at different times. Stretching and yawning dramatically and then retiring to separate rooms. But I knew. The girls, not being as watchful as me, never suspected anything. But I saw the way he looked at her and the way she looked back.

Jesse never talked about himself much. He told us that somebody he'd met in a bar on the turnpike had told him about our establishment. His only luggage was a duffel bag that bore some kind of navy insignia. I searched it while he was sleeping one night but found nothing interesting, except identification that revealed his real name. One night while Jewel was cooking dinner—she'd overcome her fear of ovens and taken to cooking since Jesse had arrived, no doubt wanting to impress him with her domestic skills—I asked him about his bag.

"Oh, that?" he said, pointing to his duffel. "That's left over from my navy days."

"What'd you do in the navy?"

"Why? You writin' a book or something, Darcy?" he asked, amused.

"No. But I make it a point of finding out about anybody who's sleeping under my roof and in my mother's bed."

"I get the feeling you don't like me much, Darcy," he said, with a laugh, "and that you don't like me staying at the inn. Am I right?"

I glared at him. "Makes no difference to me if you stay or go. The sun'll rise and set tomorrow either way."

He lit up one of the Camels he was always taking from Jewel. "Then if it's all the same to you, I think I'll stay," he said, exhaling a steady stream of smoke. "I kind of like it here."

"I bet you do. You've made yourself right at home."

"Can't blame me for that. I'm just doing what your mother

told me to do. Why the very first day I came, she says, 'Jesse, now make yourself comfortable because my house is your house.'"

"Is that so? Well, her house is also my house and just because she's weak-minded, doesn't give you the right to take advantage of her. Don't you ever intend to pay for anything? Or you planning to live off us forever?"

With the cockiness of a man who knows he's got the law on his side, Wistar Paist leaned back, blew a smoke ring, and said, "Forever is a long, long time. I don't quite look at things the way you do, Darcy. You look at me and see some man who rode in here with empty pockets looking for a handout. But the way I see it, I'm providing a service to your mother, a very valuable service that she's been wanting and waiting for a long time. And like all services, it's got to get paid for one way or another. I choose *another*."

I clenched my teeth to keep from spitting. "You're a pig!" I exclaimed heatedly. "And even saying that, I'm insulting the pig!"

Jesse stood up suddenly, his face gone red, and for a moment I thought he would hit me. I hoped he would, because hitting one of her daughters was something Jewel would never have stood for. But he recovered himself quickly enough and sat back down. "I guess I'm just going to have to live with the fact that you don't like me, Darcy."

Next day, I asked Jewel to make him leave.

"But why?" she said, looking woebegone. "He hasn't done anything."

"Not yet," I said, "but he will."

"Oh, you're always planning for the flood and seeing the worst in everybody. Jesse is just down on his luck, that's all. I don't see why you're all the time picking on him."

"I don't trust him. He's got shifty eyes."

"You don't trust anybody."

"That's right, and if we're going to survive in this world, you'd better not either."

"I won't listen to any more," she said, childishly covering both ears with her hands. "He's our guest, and I couldn't possibly ask him to leave. It'd be unkind."

I was smart enough to know when I was beat, and sharp enough to salvage what I could. "All right, Jewel. But promise me you'll never tell him about the justice's money. Not where it's hid, not even that it exists."

"Of course, I won't," she said with irritable exasperation. "Honestly, I wonder sometimes just how dumb you think I am."

"I don't think you're dumb. I just think you're...well, a bit silly when it comes to the lowlifes who wander our way."

"What do you mean, 'silly'?"

"Well, just look at the way you go riding all around the neighborhood on the back of his motorcycle, wearing his helmet. Mrs. Hennessey must be in her glory, watching you make such a fool of yourself. And with a man half your age, no less."

Jewel stared at me, piqued. "It may surprise you, missy, to learn that Jesse is twenty-seven and I am thirty-one, which doesn't exactly qualify me to be his grandma."

"Maybe not," I said, "but it should qualify you to be a decent mother and show some sense, instead of acting like you were still in the throes of puberty."

Then Jewel did something that she had never done before in my life. She slapped me, a slap that seemed to surprise her more than me, for immediately, she started to cry.

Now completely bewildered, I said, "What are *you* crying for?"

"Because I hit you," she cried, between sobs. "I never did that before, not even when you were bad and expected me to!"

"Well, there's no need to cry about it. It didn't hurt," I consoled her.

"Oh, Darcy," she said softly. "I know that I'm being a fool. But I haven't had much fun in my life. It's not that I'm complaining. I know I've been real fortunate having you and the girls with me, but being with your children, no matter how much you love them, is different from being with a man. These last few years, I've felt so old. And when Jesse came, it was like he brought youth and fun into my life. I don't suppose he'll stay forever, probably just until he gets enough money to go, or gets tired of me. But while he's here, let me enjoy him. Please. Someday you'll understand what it's like to want a man. Fate is kind and I got a feeling that destiny has picked out someone real special for you."

I looked down at my feet, suddenly ashamed. "You don't have to say more," I mumbled. "I'll try to be nice to him from now on." And I did try, and largely succeeded, though I never could bring myself to feel anything but ill will toward him.

The year that Jesse arrived was a black one all around. It was in September of that same year that Aaron Hamilton first tried to rape me. He'd always been strange, but puberty had made him unbearable. He was forever bothering the girls at school, which in itself wasn't all that odd. Most of the boys were feeling some stirrings of maleness that year, and they all teased the girls. Except for me. No one but Aaron ever teased me or conspired to brush up against me in the coat closet. Early on, I'd accepted that I wasn't pretty. Nor did I possess whatever quality it was that made boys act silly, and I didn't much care. But knowing my shortcomings all too well, I couldn't understand Aaron's pestering after me all the time.

I was stacking wood out back when I heard something rustling in the bushes nearby. Jewel was out, busy making a fool of herself riding on a motorcycle with the famous outlaw. The girls had stayed late at school to help with decorations for the annual Harvest Moon Dance. While they were too young to go, they were allowed to help decorate, so I was at home alone.

At first, I didn't pay much attention to the rustling. In the country, sounds like those are always to be heard, and it's never anything but a raccoon or a squirrel come to see what you're up to. They spy on you for a while, and when they're satisfied that it's just the usual human shenanigans, they go away again. But it wasn't a raccoon this time. This time, it was something more beastly. Aaron came out of the bushes, looking me up and down, as if I'd had on one of Jewel's satin nightgowns instead of dirty overalls.

"Long time, no see," he muttered and sat down on a tree stump. "You haven't been to school all week. How come?"

"Got things to do," I said, and went on stacking.

"Better watch out for the truant officer."

"Truant officer knows better than to—" And all of a sudden, he was right behind me, his arms locked around me, dragging me backward toward the barn. "Come inside with me," he whispered.

Aaron had the body of a boy, not a man, and under different circumstances, I'd have been more than a match for him. But he had surprise on his side. Even so, I managed to twist away and make a run for it. He charged me from behind like a bull, his thick head slamming into my back, knocking the wind out of me. He grabbed my legs and dragged me across the dirt into the barn, where he pinned me to the ground with his weight. He was having a hell of a time getting my overalls off, with me kicking and clawing at him. I didn't bother screaming, knowing that nobody was around to hear, and I was never one for wasted effort. Eventually Aaron decided to delay taking my clothes off in favor of removing his own, which were a great deal easier. When he paused to unbutton his trousers, I managed to wrench my arms free, thinking all the while that Aaron Hamilton was about to get the best of me, and I would have to continue to live in Galen, a humiliated, pitiful creature for the rest of my natural life. And then, my hand closed over the handle of a sickle hanging on the barn wall behind me. Blindly, I hurled the sickle forward, into Aaron's back. With a guttural scream, he collapsed upon me; I felt his warm blood seep through my overalls. I rolled out from under him and staggered away to the far side of the barn.

Aaron lay motionless in a pool of blood—too much for me to see just how long or deep the gash was, but it looked bad. Moving slightly, Aaron moaned, and I started to get scared. What if he bled to death right there in our barn? Murderers got the electric chair in the state of Pennyslvania. The thought propelled me out of the barn and down the road. By the time I got to Doctor Lynch's house, I was so out of breath, I could hardly say what had happened. Somehow, he pieced it together and followed me back to the barn.

It turned out the cut wasn't nearly as bad as it looked and within half an hour, the doctor had Aaron tended to and taken him home.

I didn't say a word at dinner that night and supper passed as usual with Wistar Paist and Jewel making eyes at each other, and Caroline and Jolene fighting and pinching each other under the table, for no better reason than it had become our tradition.

Just as we were finishing the meal, the knocking started; righteous knocking it was, and sure enough when Jewel opened the door, Reverend Hamilton stormed in, followed by the sheriff.

"This time that girl of yours has done it!" Hamilton roared, advancing menacingly toward Jewel. "She almost killed my boy this afternoon, nearly cut him in two."

Jewel's eyes got as big as saucers and she turned to me in disbelief. "Is that true, Darcy?"

I glanced from her to the reverend and back again. If I told about what Aaron had tried to do to me, it wouldn't have made any difference. They would do whatever it was they had come to do. And telling would just make Jewel feel bad, when it hadn't really had anything to do with her. Or maybe it really hadn't had anything to do with Aaron and me, but really only to do with Jewel and the reverend. It was all so dark and subterranean— anyway, I consoled myself, at fourteen, I was probably too young for the electric chair.

So I said, "Yep, I tried to kill him."

"Do you hear that?" The reverend pounced on my confession. "The girl doesn't even show remorse! She's a menace. I've already sent my boys away to stay with their cousins in Easton. But she'll just turn herself to enticing other boys and leading them to trouble. Just like her ma."

"What are you saying?" Jewel demanded, her mouth trembling as she put her arm around my shoulders.

"I'm saying she belongs in reform school. She's long been a truant, and today she proved herself a murderess in the making. Perhaps reform school can straighten her out."

"No!" Jewel hugged me to her. "I won't let you take my child out of this house." She looked to Jesse for support; he looked away, jamming his hands in his pockets.

"Suit yourself," Reverend Hamilton said. "But I intend to sign a complaint that she assaulted my boy and they will take her from you forcibly, if necessary."

Jewel burst into tears, but I knew crying wouldn't do any good. So I told her not to worry, that I'd be all right and would come home again real soon.

The next morning, I left. I stood for a moment at the top of the road—at the very last point where you can still see the inn, before it was lost to view—and turned back to look once more at the house. Jewel stood on the porch, alone. She waved, slow and sad, when she saw me turn, and I was struck by the notion that when I again stood on this very spot, everything would be somehow changed. The Hospitality Inn would not be the place I remembered, and Jewel would be very different from the woman I'd left. Threaded through this peculiar certainty was the feeling that something was about to be lost that would never be gotten back again. Jewel put a lot of credence in feelings. I didn't. I just turned and walked on.

I stayed at the Schuylkill County School for Wayward Girls, for three short months. Ah, dear old Schuylkill, my alma mater. I will always remember it fondly. It was just the kind of school I'd always imagined rich girls went to. We got three meals a day in a clean dining hall, and we wore neatly pressed white blouses with little collars, gray jumpers, and saddle shoes. I had never looked so nice before, nor have I since.

Every girl had a chore at Schuylkill, and the laundry—given my extensive experience—fell to me. It was easy work compared to what I had been accustomed to at the inn. In the basement of the school, great machines washed the clothes automatically, and neatly spaced clotheslines waited in the sun for the wash to be hung.

Schuylkill had a library, too, that was as big as the entire second floor of the inn. We were allowed to check out as many as three books at a time. Mrs. Gulliver, the librarian, liked me and when there was a book I liked especially, she'd let me keep it for my very own. She even let me keep the *K* volume of the encyclopedia, even though it broke up the set. That was how I learned all I could about Kathmandu, so that when I went there someday, I'd be prepared.

Sometimes I read poetry and me and Mrs. Gulliver would talk about it. Mrs. Gulliver was partial to Keats, but I thought he was a sissy. I liked Byron. He travelled more. He wrote: *For though I fly from Albion, I still can only love but one.* Albion is England, and I couldn't understand why his Lordship didn't just say England instead of confusing everyone. Mrs. Gulliver said it was probably because England doesn't rhyme with *love but one.* I wish I could have introduced Mrs. Gulliver to Leon. They'd have gotten on like a house afire with all the reciting they'd have done between them.

I was disappointed to learn that Byron had lived in England. It didn't count as travel if you already lived there. But he redeemed himself a little in my eyes when Mrs. Gulliver told me that he'd died in Greece. I was so impressed that I made up my mind then and there that I, too, would die in a foreign land far from the place of my birth.

Mrs. Gulliver had never travelled any further than Scranton to visit her sister, but I liked her just the same.

Most of all I liked living at the Schuylkill County School for Wayward Girls because I had so many friends there, especially Martha Balzell, who was in for pickpocketing, and Theresa Fimple, who'd castrated her uncle when he'd made her do things to him once too often. I'd never had any friends at home. Even my sisters were not the kind of people I'd have picked for friends. But at Schuylkill, none of my classmates had fit in at home, which was why we all fit together so well at school. I secretly hoped that I'd never finish paying my debt to society.

In fact, if not for Jewel's letters, my *bliss* would have been *unmarred*—words I had come across in poetry and in conversation with Mrs. Gulliver. I even started writing some of my own poetry. Puberty does that to people, makes them melodramatic; makes them think that they are feeling things that no one has ever thought or felt before. Byron would have been green with envy.

"Jewel, Jewel, never cruel
But oft the fool
And very messy
When it comes to men named Jesse."

(That was my first effort.)

Second effort:

"I make the concession
To the hospitality profession
For the sake of my mother
Who'll have no job other
But I'd sure prefer
To leave it to her
Get a room with a view
In the town Kathmandu."

(Well, it was better than the first.)

Mrs. Gulliver loved my poetry, which suited me fine, because at that age, I needed somebody to love something I did, even if it did stink. I guess it was her liking me that made me comfortable enough to read Jewel's letters to Mrs. Gulliver, who got a big kick out of the "creative" grammar and misspellings. Mrs. Gulliver was nice to call it "creative" instead of "stupid." She was always very charitable about ignorant people and never looked down her nose at those who hadn't had a good education.

I guess Jewel was getting scared that I was too comfortable at Schuylkill and might never come home, because every week, I'd get a letter from her:

Deer Darcy,

I miss you trebly. Plees com home. Leev that scool. You don't belong ther. We ned you and wont you bac with us.

All her letters were the same and I ignored every one of them, reading them to Mrs. Gulliver, then tucking them under my mattress. Except for the last one. That one, I never read to Mrs. Gulliver. That one, I did not keep but burned in the wash basin in my room as soon as I'd come to the end. That last letter impelled me home immediately, in the hope that it wasn't already too late.

After lights out that night, I climbed the wall, taking the possessions I'd acquired at the school—three volumes of Byron's poetry and the *K* volume of the encyclopedia. I hitched a ride from a passing farmer, then walked the last three miles to the inn. I arrived at last, footsore and weary, at two o'clock in the morning. A light burned on the inn's front porch and Jewel was pacing anxiously beneath it. She had been expecting me, knowing I would come, knowing I had never failed her and would not fail her now.

Neither one of us spoke. We didn't have to. Without a word, she led me up the back stairs to a bedroom that we used only for storage. The smell of decay hung in the hallway, heavy and oppressive. I opened the door and tried not to breathe. Jewel hung back, her hand to her mouth, shaking. I saw a shapeless form wrapped in Jewel's pink chenille bedspread; its upper end was caked with dried blood. I unwound the bedspread and exposed Jesse's face. I wrapped him up again and seized him by his boots, putting one under each arm. He may have been slight of build in life, but he was heavy as the dickens to drag once dead. Jewel backed away as I hauled his body down the hallway. Going down to the landing, his head hit each stair behind me with a sickening thud. Looking down from above, Jewel began to cry.

"Promise me," I muttered through clenched teeth.

"Anything," she sobbed.

"That we'll never talk about this. Ever."

"Don't you want to know what happened?"

"No. It can't matter now. It's done. And I never want to hear about it again, not even when we're alone. Not ever. Do you understand?"

She nodded and I went out and buried him.

Three days passed before the sheriff came. The reverend was not with him, but Mrs. Hennessey was so overcome with curiosity that she stationed herself brazenly at the bottom of the porch steps, so as to hear better. The sherriff looked surprised to see me.

"What are you doing home? I thought you were in reform school."

I shrugged. "I got reformed and they sent me back."

"Get your mother," he instructed.

"Why?"

"None of your business. Just get her and get her quick. I don't have all day. I got other business to tend to."

"Has a burst of criminal activity besieged Galen, Sheriff?" I asked.

"Get her or I'll get her myself."

"Can't."

"Why?" His body filled the doorway.

"She's ill. Influenza. Been in bed for days."

The girls came laughing into the parlor behind me. I chased them out, so that the sheriff wouldn't have a chance to ask them anything. I could have told them what to say, rehearsed them till they got it right, but they weren't really a part of the secret. It was between me and Jewel and no one else. Besides, there was no use in involving them. They had slept right through it all and couldn't know what had happened. "Maybe I can help you," I volunteered. "I'm handling Jewel's affairs while she's sick."

He hesitated. "All right. You know that fella called hisself Jesse James?"

"Of course, I know him. He lived in my house goin' on a year."

"Well, his name isn't Jesse James at all."

"No?" I asked breathlessly.

"That's right. Real name's Wistar Paist and the government is looking for him."

"What for?"

"Seems Paist went AWOL in Philadelphia right after his ship docked. He's in a lot of trouble."

"Well, he isn't here if that's what you came for."

"I didn't think he was. Highway patrol found his motorcycle abandoned on the highway. Seems odd he'd just go off and leave it like that."

"Maybe somebody offered him a ride," I said helpfully.

"When did he leave here, Darcy?"

"Yesterday, maybe around two o'clock."

"Is he coming back?"

"I doubt it," I said. "You know how his kind are, first one place, then another."

"Why'd he leave?" he asked me. "I thought that things was real cozy with your mama and him, just holed up here like two bugs in a rug."

I forced myself not to sound offended. "I told you all I know. He left because that's the kind of man he is, a drifter. Men like that never stay in one place long."

The sheriff removed his hat and leaned against the porch post. "I get the feeling you're hiding something. Maybe you're hiding him. Maybe you got him in the attic or the barn."

"You're welcome to search the house, if it'll make you sleep better," I said, throwing the door wide.

"I'm not that stupid," he muttered scornfully. "I'm sure your stalling has given him plenty of time to escape. We'll search the orchard and the woods. Maybe he's hiding there just waiting for you to give the all clear sign."

My throat went dry. I had buried Jesse in the orchard where the earth was soft. And nothing, I knew, aroused canine curiosity like the combination of death and soft earth. Old Sam had tried to dig him back up, and if the sheriff had brought dogs....

"I couldn't help but overhear," Mrs. Hennessey interjected,

climbing the porch steps, as if to take her place at center stage. "Darcy is speaking the truth. That Mr. James did go off just like Darcy said. Why, I'm probably the last person in Galen to see him go," she said triumphantly, as if expecting a prize. Clearly, she now thought herself an indispensable part of the conversation.

"You saw him, Mrs. Hennessey? When was that?"

"Well," she deliberated. "It must have been about two, because the sun was just beginning to go down down over the ridge. Mr. James was walking along the ridge, swinging that duffel bag of his. Mr. Hennessey used to have one of those when he was in the navy, God rest his soul. He waved to me from up on the ridge, Mr. James, I mean, not Mr. Hennessey, who's been dead for thirty years, and couldn't possibly wave."

"Was he wearing the black helmet, ma'am?"

"Now let me just think." The widow put a bony finger to her lips. "Yes, yes, he was."

"Then are you sure it was him? It's pretty far up to the top of that ridge, and with a helmet on…"

"I'm positive," she snapped, clearly affronted at the notion she might have been mistaken. "I saw him just as clear as I see you standing here. My eyes are as sharp as ever, and it was that James fellow up on that ridge. Just because I'm getting old doesn't mean I can't see."

"All right now, ma'am. There's no need to get your bowels in an uproar. If you say it was him, it was him. Just seems strange, that's all."

"Are you satisfied now?" I demanded.

"For the time being," the sheriff answered. "But you and your mama better stick around, 'cause there's something about this whole thing that smells like old fish."

"And where would I possibly go?" I asked defiantly. "Nobody in Galen ever goes anywhere except to the cemetery."

And, feeling sad in a way that had nothing to do with the dead man in the orchard, I went back into the house.

3

Lighting a Little Hour or Two

In the history of mankind, has there ever been a life that went according to plan? At sixteen, I had my entire life, as well as the entire lives of my sisters, all planned out in advance. It seemed the practical thing to do.

The girls were shaping up nicely. Jolene was getting smarter every day and dazzling us all with her book knowledge. And Caroline took your breath away with her overwhelming beauty, though she was somewhat more overwhelmed than the rest of us. But I wasn't fooled. Despite their sterling qualities, they were as self-sufficient as chicks in a fox den, and I knew that they would never really be able to take care of themselves. Hence, somebody would have to always be there to take care of them, and I was damned if it was going to be me. The only logical persons to assume responsibility for them in later life, since they would never do it themselves, were husbands. Better yet, rich husbands who would have the means to shelter them from the harsher aspects of life, just as Jewel and I had done. I reasoned that there was only one place where a young girl could count on meeting, if not wealthy, then at least up and coming men, and that was college, which everyone knew was jam-packed with rising doctors and lawyers. For myself, I didn't regret that I would never go to college because I knew I would always know more about the things that counted than my teachers. It would have been nice to marry Jewel off, too, but that wasn't likely, seeing as how she'd been on the market so long already with no takers.

As for me, I planned never to marry. The idea of loving somebody seldom crossed my mind except in the most fleeting way. I loved Jewel and my sisters simply because I'd taken care of them for so long, and when you put a lot of care into something, you grow to love it, even if you didn't start out that way.

Loving a man never occurred to me at all. I knew you needed one to have a baby, but you needed him for such a short time, just a minute or two probably, that it seemed pointless to sign up for a lifetime of service. Besides, I didn't much like children. They were too loud and bothersome and tied you down for half your life—the good half—so that you never got to travel anywhere and wound up born and dead in the same lousy little town. Not for me. The only kind of future that I would even consider was one filled with adventure, with no sisters and no Jewel depending on me for everything from lighting ovens to fixing the truck.

Nobody gets to pick where they're born or who they're born to, and I accepted my lot in life early on, but as soon as the girls went away to college and Jewel had mastered the basic principles of profitable innkeeping, I was going. I'd point myself in the direction of Kathmandu and little by little, town by town, year by year, I'd get closer to it. Maybe I wouldn't reach my destination till I was an old, old woman, but damn it to hell if I was about to let anybody hang on my coattails when time came to start the journey, not even the people I loved. Loving someone, I'd determined, would only slow me down and delay my travels to exotic places. And many years would pass before I came to know that the place where you love a man deeply and irrevocably is the most exotic place to be found.

It's strange how we never recognize the future, how the most momentous things can happen, and for a while we go along thinking nothing's changed at all. That's how it was with him.

I was out back when I heard somebody coming up the walk. I'd been busy all morning butchering a pig, a job I hated, but since I was fond of eating regular, I'd reconciled myself to the slaughter. I reminded myself that we prey upon and are preyed upon. That's just how it is. My hands were all bloody when I came around front, wiping them on my apron. An old man waited there, with a young boy hovering behind. I waited for the old fellow to say something, but he just stood dumbfounded, staring at my bloody apron. Finally, he lifted his eyes and in broken English, he muttered something and pointed up to the house. I didn't understand his words but figured he wanted a room at the Hospitality Inn. Jewel had recently painted a sign that read: "George Washington Slept Here," in the hope of attracting foreigners, and I wondered if this idiocy had actually worked. I felt sure that whatever money these foreigners had, if they had any at all, would quickly run out, and they would become one of our Special Discount guests.

I gave the old guy a good once over. He was sick. I could tell by the yellow in his eyes where there should have been white, by the ashen pallor of his face, and the trembling of his limbs. He barely had the strength to stand and leaned heavily on the boy, breathing shallowly. I was about to tell him no when Jewel came out of the house in a lather. Some clairvoyance informing her that I was just about to boot a vagrant off our property. She came down the steps like lady bountiful with a big broad smile, and took the old man's hand, shaking it vigorously as if she were queen of England and he some visiting prince. Taking her aside, I asked, "Are you out of your mind, crazy woman? That man has got a sickness as sure as I live and breathe, and it could very well be catching and then we'll all sicken and die. And I'll be damned if I'll nurse that old goat and expose myself to what could be black plague or something worse."

"My father is not ill," the boy stated in perfect, if heavily accented, English. "He is only tired. We have been travelling for many weeks."

I held the boy's gaze—his eyes dark blue, his expression haughty and proud. Neither of us blinked, and we might have gone on a long time like that, if Jewel hadn't spoken. "How do you come to be here?" she asked, and he shifted his gaze to her.

"We came to New York from Italy and then into Pennsylvania. My father has a brother in the next town, but when we arrived there, he was gone. We knew not where. Our money is not much and the hotels in other places are very dear. A man we meet when we stop to get water tells us to come here. He says he has been here once, and there is a woman who will help us." I almost laughed out loud when he said that, as if Jewel were some great abolitionist hiding colored people on their way to Canada.

The boy smiled at Jewel, revealing dimpled cheeks and even white teeth. I wasn't impressed and made a great effort to show I wasn't. Jewel, on the other hand, was pleased as punch at having her reputation precede her, and before I could put my foot down, she was leading the two up the steps and into the parlor, leaving me to go back to my butchering with renewed vigor and fit to be tied.

That night, Jewel insisted we cook the pig. I'd been hoping to save it until the strangers were gone. It wasn't easy raising it or butchering it, and I wasn't about to share it with people I didn't even know. But Jewel said that would be rude and served it up anyhow.

For a sick man, that old Eye-talian sure could eat. I watched every piece that disappeared into his mouth, wishing I could pull it back up his throat. The boy, in contrast, ate hardly anything, and I got the feeling he was trying to make up for the other's gluttony.

Cursing every moment, I made up two beds in adjoining rooms. When I'd finished, I asked Jewel in my most sarcastic tone if she wanted me to tuck them in and read them a fairy story as well.

Next morning, Jewel cajoled me into bringing the old goat his breakfast in bed. I fumed plenty, but in the end, I gave in because she promised I could throw them out in two weeks if they didn't pay.

Being disgruntled made the tray heavy and I lumbered up the steps as if it weighed a hundred pounds. Knocking at the door, I waited. No answer. I put my ear to the door and knocked again. Opening the door a crack, I made out the curve of the old man's back beneath the blanket. Nudging the door open with my foot, I deposited the tray on the bureau. "Good morning!" I said brightly. Then, walking around the other side of the bed, I stopped short. I knew immediately that he was dead. I felt his neck for a pulse. There was none. I raised his wrist and let go. It flopped on the bed. The man was dead, and I was madder than ever at Jewel for letting him stay the night. Now who the hell was going to take him away? I'd be damned if I'd be the one to drag him downstairs. Damn Jewel. Why hadn't she listened to me when I told her he was sick? He wasn't family after all. We weren't responsible for him. He could have gone to a nice comfortable hotel somewhere and dropped dead in luxury.

"He's dead!" I hissed at Jewel when I got back downstairs. "He's dead and piss, shit, hell, damn, what are we supposed to do with him now?"

Her lips quivered like they always did when I yelled at her. "Are you sure?"

"I know the quick from the dead, Jewel!"

She looked at me helplessly. "I just thought maybe he wasn't completely dead."

"Jesus H. Christ. He's as dead as dead can be."

She wrung her hands. "How are you going to tell his boy?"

I could have slapped her. "How am *I* going to tell him? I'm not telling anybody anything. You're the one's gonna march up there and tell him. You're the one loves to minister to the sick and disheartened."

"Oh, please, Darcy," she said in her most plaintive manner. "If you tell him, I promise never to take in any strangers again."

I knew she was lying through her teeth and she knew I knew because she avoided my gaze and said, "But you know I'm no good at this kind of thing."

I folded my arms. "Neither am I. And isn't it you who's always said that death isn't nothing to be afraid of? That it's no more than just passing through a door? Well, go tell that boy upstairs that his father just took himself through the door."

It never really did any good to try to resist Jewel. She had a peculiar magnetism that could always charm you into doing what she wanted, and the few times that didn't work, she had no aversion to begging. A little later, I was knocking at the boy's door, trying to think of a kind way to say, "Your father's dead, so don't look for him in this lifetime ever again."

He opened the door sleepily, rubbing his eyes. He was bare-chested and wore the pants he'd had on the night before. He turned clear and questioning blue eyes on me.

"Here's your breakfast," I told him, placing the plate on his bedside table. "You hardly ate anything last night. You must be hungry. Go ahead and eat. I'll wait to take the tray back."

He sat on the edge of the bed, looking suspiciously at the food, then at me, as if I'd poisoned his breakfast. I watched him taste the oatmeal and even though his expression didn't change, I could tell he didn't like it. But he ate everything while I tried to gather my thoughts. He looked haggard and weary, as if he'd scarcely slept. He had a long straight nose and a delicate mouth, and if not for his square chin, he'd have looked feminine. But even the chin couldn't make up for the long black eyelashes and the dimples. There was no getting away from it—he was almost as pretty as Caroline, and I thought he looked like a right sissy.

My eyes dropped down to the rest of him. Not the body of a man, nor that of a boy, but somewhere in between. "Your father's pretty old, isn't he?" I said abruptly.

"Old?" he asked with a frown. "Not so old. Perhaps fifty years or so. Hard work has made him seem older than he is."

I opened my mouth to speak when I realized that I didn't know his name. "What's your name?"

"I am called Luca," he answered patiently. "Luca D'Angeli."

"Luca," I repeated. "That's a funny name. And you're from Italy. Is that anywhere near Kathmandu?"

"No."

"Oh," I said, disappointed. "We've never had any Eye-talian people around here before. How old are you?"

"Sixteen. How old are you?"

"Seventeen," I said and watched his eyes widen.

"Seventeen? But your hair—?"

Suddenly aware of the gray in my hair, I stammered, "How come you speak English so good?"

He swelled up some when I said that. "My father and I always knew that one day we would come to America, and knowing this, I studied very hard to prepare myself. But when we get to New York, a doctor says we must go back because my father is sick. He makes an *X* on my father's coat and says that sick people cannot come to America."

"What did you do?"

"I tell him that my father is not sick, only tired. The doctor looks in his eyes and ears and mouth and then says it is all right. We can leave the boat. He is not so sick."

"Hmmm. Maybe they were right the first time."

Luca looked at me blankly.

"Look," I said, "I don't know how to tell you this except straight out. Your father died during the night." I couldn't help feeling a little annoyed that he hadn't guessed and spared me the awkwardness of having to tell him.

For a moment, Luca just stared at me, expressionless. Then he covered his face with his hands and started to cry.

I had never seen a man cry before, and I was embarrassed for both of us. Watching him, I felt a little sad, too, but reminded myself that it was his father and not mine who had died—and that the dead old man and his crying boy were both strangers to me. Like our other boarders, they would come and go, bringing nothing with them when they came and leaving nothing behind when they went (except for Leon, who'd left the truck, the *Rubaiyat*, and the gun; and Duncan, who'd left Caroline and Jolene). Just the same, it was uncomfortable to see him carry on like this, and I hoped he'd stop soon. I reached out to touch his shoulders that shuddered with his sobbing, but at the last minute changed my mind.

"It isn't like he got hit by a truck," I said, trying to comfort him. "He lived, grew old—fifty is old—and died in his sleep. It was real natural. I should be so lucky."

Luca didn't answer me and when, finally, he had calmed

himself enough to speak, it was more to himself than to me. "My father must have been sick all along," he said, wiping his eyes. "He must have held on just long enough to see that I got here safely."

"I s'pose," I said, trying to be agreeable. "What do you want to do with the body?"

"The body?" he repeated dully. "Yes, his body. I must go and prepare him." With that he stood up and went into the adjoining room, closing the door behind him. With my ear to the thin wood, I could hear the sound of running water and the creaking of bed springs. He was washing his father's body, though I couldn't for the life of me imagine why. Once you were dead, what difference did it make if you were dirty or clean? Why get spiffed up for kingdom come?

Jewel came up with Old Sam at her heels. The dog sniffed the doorframe, and I wondered if dogs could smell death and what it smelled like to them. Cooked cabbage, I guessed. About half an hour passed before Luca came out. He closed the door softly behind him, then stood before Jewel and me looking down at the floor uncomfortably.

"Sometimes, Luca, honey, you just got to leave it where Jesus flung it," Jewel offered cryptically, doing little to make an awkward situation any easier.

I wanted to know what he planned to do with his father's body, and how soon he would be vacating his room. What he did after that and where he went, I didn't know or want to know.

Predictably, Jewel put a hand on his arm. "Come, sit downstairs for a moment," she said, leading him gently down the hallway to the sitting room below. Once Luca had been settled in an armchair to her satisfaction, she asked, "Do you want us to take care of the funeral arrangements?"

Aware where this was leading, I gritted my teeth, shooting her what I hoped was a discouraging glare. Luca's eyes hung on Jewel as if she were all that kept him afloat.

"We haven't much money," Jewel told him to my relief, "but whatever we have, you're welcome to."

That was the last straw. “But—but that money is for the girls’ college education!” I blurted out.

Luca gave me a look that would have withered me if I were capable of being withered. “My father brought money,” he said. “Not a lot of money, but enough to bury him. I would not take money from women,” he added with a stiff pride.

“Shame on you, Darcy,” Jewel said.

But Luca looked bewildered. “Shame? She has no reason for shame. It is right she thinks of her family first.”

“There’s the family of man too,” Jewel told him. It was just the kind of thing she would say, and mad at them both—Jewel for crossing me, Luca for defending me—I folded my arms and turned away.

Luca clearly understood Jewel’s pronouncement no better than I did because from the corner of my eye, I saw him watching her mouth like a deaf man, trying to figure out what she was saying from her moving lips. “And after the funeral,” she went on, unruffled because she was used to being misunderstood, “what then? Do you have family back in Italy?”

My ears perked up, like Old Sam’s when something stirred in the brush. This was more in keeping with my plans.

“I have an aunt and uncle there and a few cousins, but after I pay to bury my father, I won’t have enough money to return. I wish very much that I had enough money to bring my father to Italy and bury him there.”

“What’s wrong with here?” I interrupted, feeling somehow slighted. “Galen’s a great place to be buried. Sometimes, I think that’s all it’s a great place for.”

“I don’t know what to do,” Luca told Jewel, ignoring me. “Perhaps it would be wrong to go back to Italy. My father sacrificed everything for us to come here.”

Jewel patted his hand. “I don’t think your father would have wanted you to go back. I think he’d have wanted you to stay with us for a while.”

I choked on my breakfast, and Jewel pounded me on the back as I coughed and spluttered.

"No, I could not stay here," Luca replied. "I would be a burden."

Because I could not speak for coughing, I nodded vigorously to show I concurred.

"No, no," Jewel insisted. "We could use a man's help around here, especially a big, strong boy like you."

"Perhaps I could find work," Luca said hesitantly. "Just for a short while."

Jewel laughed. "Honey, if you try and take work away from the men in Galen, especially you being foreign and all, you're just likely to wind up seeing your father again sooner than you think. Besides, you're just a boy. You should be in school. In the meantime, you could be a big help to us just doing things around the inn. I know Darcy needs you."

My mouth fell open in protest, but Jewel was already pushing me toward the door.

Two days later, Jewel badgered me and the girls into putting on our good clothes and going to the funeral, where she and the boy stood together crying like professional mourners. His wailing I could understand. He was Eye-talian after all, and the man had been his father. But hers? She had known the old man less than five waking hours. How aggrieved could she be? It was galling the way she was forever bringing trouble into the house, while I was forever trying to keep it out. It wasn't our tragedy after all. But as with everything else, Jewel never could tell the difference as to where she left off and other folks began.

So gradually, almost inevitably, did Luca D'Angeli work his way into our lives that before many months had passed, it seemed he had always been with us, as much a part of the Hopsitality Inn as the old weather vane on the roof that had belonged to the Justice's grandmother. Or rather, it seemed that way to the others.

To me, there was nothing right about him being with us, and I resented his presence more and more every day. For one thing, he was so damned helpful, it made me want to scream. Wherever, I was working—in the yard, house, barn, or orchard—he was there, waiting to take the hoe or the axe or the scrub brush from my hand. He was trying to replace me in my own house, and the others were happy to let him.

Everybody liked him, liked him better than they did me. He talked with Jolene by the hour about two Eye-talians named Dante and Beatrice, and they completely ignored me when I tried to tell how Byron had died in Greece, far from the land of his birth.

Jewel doted on him as if he were her own son, but worst of all was Caroline, who surely had the makings of a tart. She flirted outrageously with him and lacked the decency to try to hide it. Being short, she'd look up at him with those china-blue eyes in the most adoring way, and he'd beam down at her, showing his dimples. It was all I could do to keep food down. Needless to say, he never looked at me like that. I was just as tall as him and could look him in the eye, and it's a rare man who can stand that. Once, when Caroline was trying to reach something high in the cupboard, she apologized for her limitations, then coyly asked Luca to retrieve it for her. Her apology was insincere, I knew, because Caroline enjoyed being small. It made it easier to get people to do things for her. Luca shrugged off her apology and said that there was an old Eye-talian saying: "Tall girls are only good for picking fruit." When he turned and saw that I had heard, he blushed and turned away.

I put up with this throughout the long summer, but I knew, come autumn, I'd have my revenge when classes started, and Galen high schoolers got a look at this foreign boy. They'd take him down a notch or two.

But it never happened. Luca's classmates were standoffish instead of hostile, and even that turned quickly to a warm indifference and then to aloof affection. Through Caroline, who soaked up gossip like a sponge, I learned that just about all the girls in Galen thought Luca was good-looking, that the boys liked him because he was good at games, and even the teachers liked him because he was so damned smart with books and could outshine almost all the natives. And it was this ability to make people like him that, more than anything else, settled my determination to rid myself and my household of his presence forever.

Things changed somehow at the inn after he came, and try as I might, they wouldn't change back. Every night at dinner, Jewel would ask Luca and the girls about the events of the school day. Luca would proceed to regale them with stories of very ordinary everyday things, yet he managed to make them seem more interesting than they were, and everyone would laugh and beg him to tell more. Everyone but me.

Life was a serious business and having a court jester in residence didn't change that. It wasn't that I wanted dinner to be grave, but I would have liked to talk about what we should plant that year, or if we should plant anything at all in view of all my past failures to coax anything out of our rocky dirt. I wanted to talk about how we could make more money and whether it would be worth it to get a new wood stove. But the dinner conversation never got more serious than talk about how Miss Beehall's bloomers showed when she bent down to pick up chalk.

Why everybody was so willing to provide an audience to his bragging, I had no idea. Maybe he was smart—almost smart as Jolene, maybe even smarter in his own language—but did he have to be such a know-it-all? When he first went to school, I'd decided to say yes when he asked me for help with his homework. I was a year his senior, after all. But he never asked. In fact, sometimes he used English words that I didn't understand. So I was reduced to using words peculiar to Galen, so he wouldn't understand. But even that satisfaction was short-lived. He was as quick to pick up Galen-talk as he'd been to learn French, German, and Spanish. I couldn't trust a boy who spoke five languages. It just wasn't natural, and it was just one more thing about him that kept me from liking him.

Then in the spring, I finally found someone who didn't like Luca. His name was Joseph Gibbet and he stayed with us only one night on his way to New Hampshire. Board was always included with a room at the Hospitality Inn and so we sat down to dinner together. Our guest ate like a hog and didn't say a word until he'd finished his dinner. But then he leaned back and lit a pipe and waxed playful. He said he was headed to New Hampshire, because he had found work there and dared us to guess his livelihood. He bet us a dollar that we'd never be able to guess, which set us all to pondering. Clearly, he wasn't a coal miner or a railroad man. We demanded hints, and he cheerfully provided some. He travelled often; there was little enough work in any one state to keep him there for long. In many states, he was prohibited by law from working at all; in others, other people had the same job but did it in a different manner. There was a lot of measuring required to do it right and it involved climbing steps. Even when he didn't perform his job particularly well, no one complained. "Give up?" he asked, gleeful as a small child. We all gave up, Jewel and the girls because they couldn't figure it out, me because I never saw the sense in giving effort to something that would not substantially profit me or mine.

"I don't give up," Luca told him haughtily. "Give me one more clue."

Joseph Gibbet tapped out his pipe, annoyed. "Pretty sure of yourself for a foreigner with no right reason to be in these parts." Luca's face was impassive. "...but all right...my name. My name's a clue."

Joseph Gibbet, Joseph Gibbet, Joseph Gibbet, I repeated to myself silently. I thought it was a silly sounding name and wondered if he had a silly job.

"You are a hangman," Luca stated. Gibbet's face contorted with rage and for a moment I thought he might stamp his foot through the floor like Rumpelstiltskin.

When moments passed and nothing was said, Jewel finally spoke: "Well? Is he right?"

"Yes," Gibbet said grudgingly.

"Have you hanged anybody in Pennsylvania?" I asked.

The others looked at me. Jewel had often said I was morbid, and maybe that was true, but I couldn't help being curious.

"Nah, they give 'em the 'lectric chair now. But my father hanged a man here in Schuylkill County back in '11, and my grandfather some more back in the days when hangings was public the way they should be. Now it's all hush-hush behind prison walls. Takes all the joy out of it."

"Joy?" Jewel said, frowning.

"That's right. The joy of knowing I'm riddin' society of the scum of the earth. Man I'm on my way to hang now in Concord killed a ten-year-old boy—did things to him first, if you know what I'm getting at. World's got no use for somebody like that, and I'm proud of what I do. There's an art to it too. Not many folks realize that. 'Course I have to depend on the wardens not to let the bastards cheat me and hang themselves before I can git there. Then, when I do, I set up my own scaffold—don't trust nobody's but my own—and I measure 'em. They gotta fall just so many feet and not further. Otherwise the head pops off and makes the witnesses vomit. Happened to my grandfather long time ago. And it was a woman yet. If you measure right and they're lucky, the neck breaks and it's over quick. But sometimes God seems to want to extract a special punishment and the neck don't break, like the man back in '11. Noose slipped around the back of his neck and he was strangled. That can take minutes. Don't bother me. I got no place else I have to be. But it ain't too pleasant for him."

"You owe Luca a dollar," Jewel said coldly. She seemed to feel that was quite enough for us to know about hanging. "He earned it."

"The hell he did! He asked for an extra clue. That's cheating."

I hadn't often seen Jewel angry and I was surprised to see her so then, and over something so ridiculous as guessing an occupation. "Give that boy his dollar or get out of my house!" she said, and he wouldn't and he went, and that was the first and the last time I ever met a hangman. When I look back on that evening, I wonder if it was Jewel thinking of the orchard and who was buried there that made her so inhospitable to Joe Gibbet, never mind the dollar bet. I also think that Luca really had earned the dollar, because Gibbet never said anything about a player being disqualified for asking for a final clue. The rules should be made clear before the game begins if it's to be fair and that's, at bottom, why life's unfair. You just get thrust into the game whether you want to play or not and without being made aware of the rules, which you only come to understand later when it's already too late.

That summer was godawful. Hot as hell and making people mean—and by people, I of course mean me. Then September came and with it that peculiar exhilaration that comes with the first chill. At dusk, my favorite time of day, I used to sit out on my porch in my wicker chair all by myself. Jewel and the girls knew I liked to be alone with nobody but Old Sam, asleep under my chair, for an hour until the sun went down. It was really the only way I indulged myself and they knew better than to disturb my solitude or try to join me. Being around people all day and having to listen to them and respond to them, even if they are your family, can be exhausting. Being alone for that short time was my way of reconciling myself to the sociability that dinner would again demand of me. Only once did anyone bother me and that was when the stove caught fire, and even then, Jewel came out real timid of approach and only after all attempts to bribe Jolene and Caroline into getting me had failed.

What I thought about when I was sitting out on my porch was, I knew, an enduring mystery to everybody. I'd just sit there rocking, gazing out across the fields, past the broken fence to where the land sloped up and away, to the dense foliage of trees and shrubs. Everything was so still, so perfectly still at that hour, that the quiet was like a balm on all the day's scrapes. I liked the smells of autumn, the decay of what weeks before had been at its peak, the hay bales lying in the field, the smoke of a distant burning. And I liked to think about things, things that had happened and things that maybe would. My family would have been shocked to know the plans I made, plans that never included them. Someday I would travel to places they could not imagine. Exotic and savage places. I would send them postcards. (I'd gotten a postcard once. From Mrs. Gulliver who'd gone to Pittsburgh for three days.) Sometimes, I could see myself so clearly, with suitcase in hand, poised to step on a boat or a train, and my heart would start to beat real fast, so fast it slammed against my ribs, and I'd have to put my hand on my chest to make it stop. Then my hour would be up, and a voice belonging to its own time would call me in. But for that hour, no one dared to intrude on my private wanderings and wonderings—except for Luca.

He'd walk right up onto my porch as bold as brass and plop himself down in the chair beside me. "*Come sta*, Darcy?" he'd say, just so as to be annoying. And I would always shoot back, "Speak English!"

His dimples would retreat into a frown. "Why have you been away from school for so many monse?"

"Months," I would correct him. For all his linguistic prowess, some sounds still announced that he was no native. "And you won't see me in school for many more monse, so stop looking." I gave him a sideways glance. "Besides, not all of us are as popular as you, and not all of us want to go to that stupid hillbilly school for stupid hillbillies."

He laughed, unoffended. "I should teach you to speak Italian. Then you could be sarcastic in two languages."

"There's nothing you can teach me. I'm older than you, and I know more."

"Only one year," he said. "I know something I could teach you. I could teach you how to hunt, how to use that shotgun you have in the barn."

"How do you know about that?" I demanded.

"I saw it there. Why? Is the gun a secret?" he whispered, as if willing to be a part of the conspiracy.

"No. I know how to hunt just fine."

"You don't. I mean you could probably hit an elephant if it agreed to stay still long enough. But I mean deer, squirrel, something you could eat."

I hesitated and hesitation is weakness.

"Tomorrow we will get up before the sun," he said, "and we'll walk until we find a proper place."

I didn't say anything. Not then. Not all through dinner that evening. I did not want to go with him. I did not need to learn anything from him. I did not like his company. I particularly did not want to be alone with him. And yet, when he came down the next morning wearing all the clothes he owned because it was a very cold morning and still dark, I was waiting for him. And if you had asked me why, I would not have been able to answer. Not then. Not yet.

We walked north. I didn't know what we were looking for and didn't want to ask him. So I just walked behind him and observed the silence. It was the only time I ever remember walking behind him and it felt natural and uncomfortable at the same time.

Finally, he stopped and pointed to a ridge. "See that? That's a natural funnel, a space between the mountain and the road. The deer can't get to the creek without passing this way."

I nodded and he took my arm, leading me to a thicket where we crouched down behind the thick trunk of a fallen tree. "Keep your ears above the trunk or you won't be able to hear them approach," he said. "This gun only shoots one bullet at a time. We'll only have one chance. If we miss, the animal will be in Wilkes Barre before we can reload. I'll hand the gun to you when the deer's in sight. You look down the barrel and squeeze very slowly. Now all you have to do is listen and be very quiet. No talking." He laughed a little in anticipation of his own joke. "I know you can go without talking, sometimes for days on end."

We sat there for what seemed like hours. My fingers and toes had long since lost feeling, and I was just starting to wonder whether they might be lost to amputation when I heard a faint rustling. Luca's hand gripped my thigh in a quick squeeze, then swiftly, silently he pivoted the gun to his left so that his face, staring down the barrel, was so close to my own that I could feel his breath on my eyelashes. Something happened to me in that moment. I felt a rush of warmth, where I had been freezing only moments before and I wondered vaguely if that was a sign of frostbite. My heart pounded in my ears, as if I'd been winded from running, and my head swam. Time slowed or stopped or simply wasn't—I can't explain it any better than that—but I could look at him as if from a distance, though his face was mere inches from mine, and I thought how very beautiful he was, more like a painting or a sculpture of a man than a man himself and how fine his hands were, not coarse like farmers' hands but not soft either, just perfectly formed hands. Then, as if it were coming to me in a dream, I felt him pressing the gun on me and murmuring, "Squeeze slowly." But my arms were heavy and limp and I could not lift them to take the weapon. A gunshot sounded so close to my ear that I was deafened. I felt his shoulders heave back from the recoil, and he lowered the gun. "He's going to run. He's dead. He just doesn't know it yet." Luca motioned me to follow him and I did. "He's looking for a place to die. We must allow him that much. All we have to do is follow the blood trail."

Luca walked with his eyes to the ground. I supposed there was blood there and I supposed we were following it, but I couldn't say for sure because my eyes were fixed upon him, held there by some mysterious gravitational pull like the moon on the tides.

We found the buck in a sheltered spot under a thicket. A hunter who could not read the signs of its flight would have never found it. Luca took a knife from his belt and cut the animal from throat to tail, then reached his hands within its body and removed organs that steamed in the cold air, all the while keeping up a narration of anatomy: "Heart, the best to eat....liver...intestines, we'll make sausage..." When the entrails had been deposited in an old feed sack he'd brought for this purpose, he tied a length of rope around the buck's antlers and handed me the sack with the entrails. We made our way out of the woods and back home, him dragging the deer and me walking behind him carrying the sack still dripping blood.

I'm not sure exactly when, but at some point, on our walk home, I felt a fury rising within me. I had no valid reason to be so angry at him, but the invalid one I had was this: We had gone into the woods and killed a deer and were returning with it. That much we could have agreed on if called to account for our time that day. But other than these skeletal facts, we might as well have spent the day across the world from each other, so different it seemed had been our experience. The woods had changed me. I felt as if some kind of communion had taken place. For me. Not for him. The woods had not changed him. And because I had never had time to brood on anything, so immediate and urgent always were the demands of basic human comfort, I did not question myself further. I knew only that I could not risk my eyes meeting his ever again.

When we got home, it was already dark. Luca displayed his kill proudly and the girls and Jewel *oohed* and *aahed* over the buck. Jewel declared she'd nail the antlers over the mantel, and Luca proclaimed he'd cook the heart and liver for dinner. Everybody went into the kitchen to watch, but I resisted, saying I had no appetite and was going to sit on the porch for a spell. Jewel protested that it was too cold, but I snapped that it was nearly the shortest day of the year and the stars were more brilliant than ever and worth watching from my porch rocker. This was the last thing I should have said, because they all joined me.

"Let's all go out and watch the stars," Luca said. "I'll put the meat on to simmer and come." Jewel and the girls piled on coats and hats and came out with Luca a few minutes after. He sat on the porch steps as far away from me as possible, so maybe he had sensed something of my discomfort. It never occurred to me that he was feeling a discomfort of his own. Jewel sat near the railing and Jolene next to her. Old Sam, faithful even in the bitter cold, took up his usual spot at my feet and every so often, I'd bend down to scratch his ears. He was the only member of my household with whom I felt truly at peace. Caroline sat herself next to Luca, looking pert and pretty in a blue hat she'd knitted for herself. The color matched her eyes and she knew it.

For a while, none of us talked but for Caroline and Luca, who murmured between themselves. I wasn't paying much attention to their talk until I heard him say, "...then you'll go to the Christmas dance with me?"

"I'd like that," Caroline replied, so coyly I could have slapped her face till feeling came back in my fingers. "But you'll have to ask Jewel."

Luca glanced at Jewel, but before she could open her mouth, I said, "Caroline is too young to be going out with boys, especially foreign boys. Besides, I've seen Luca panting after Cathleen Haddock with his tongue hanging around his ankles."

"Darcy!" Jewel rushed to his defense. "Luca's love life is his own business."

I folded my arms across my chest and started rocking furiously. "That's true. It's his pecker, and I suppose it's his business where he puts it." Luca blushed down to his hair line.

"Darcy, shush. You're embarrassing him."

"Oh, shush yourself. It's true and you know it. He'll have his fun with Caroline and then he'll go back to Italy and marry some Eye-talian virgin with purple feet and a moustache."

"That's not fair," Jewel said. "I trust Luca like family, and I'd be proud to have him take your sister to the dance." Caroline was beaming, but Luca didn't seem to be feeling triumphant.

"How can you know who to trust?" I said back. "Every derelict comes down the road is family to you."

"I can just tell," Jewel insisted stubbornly, and the porch was silent for a while.

Jolene was the one to break the quiet. She sighed loud and long. "I wish I was old enough to start college. I can do all the high school work. I'm bored to tears with it." (Jolene went through life generally bored and would eventually become bored with boredom. But then it wasn't easy being the smartest person in the world.)

"You just be patient, little girl," Jewel told her. "You and Caroline will both go to college. Darcy will fix it." Her brow furrowed. "Somehow, I don't know how, but she'll fix it so you can go." I harrumphed. She'll fix it, indeed—just as it was with the fixing of the stove, or the mending of the fence, or the hiding of the bodies. *Darcy would fix it.*

Luca leaned back against the porch post. He never added much to conversations, at least not while I was around. His eyes came to rest on me. "And you, Darcy. What will you do?"

Startled to have him direct words at me, I looked back at him, or more accurately, a fraction to the left of him. But I didn't have a chance to reply before Caroline piped up: "They'll have to take old Darcy out of here in a box. She'll never leave any other way." Caroline hardly ever said anything remotely clever and she giggled, pleased with herself to no end.

I gave her the evil eye. "You're mighty lucky to be sitting out of my reach, little sister. That's all you know about it anyhow. Won't you be taken aback when you get my postcards from faraway places."

"Sure thing, Darcy," Jolene joined in. "As far away as Scranton, I'll bet."

Everyone laughed, except for Luca. I tried to read his face, but he leaned back into the darkness of the porch where the winter moon's light didn't penetrate.

"You can all go to hell!" I exclaimed angrily, but that only amused the girls all the more, so I quit the porch and left them laughing at me.

It was real surprising the next day to find out that Reverend Hamilton had hanged himself in his own house. Or I should say, all of us, excepting Luca and Jewel, were surprised; Luca, because he had never met the reverend; and Jewel, who just nodded when I told her, as if it was something she'd been expecting all along. I just couldn't figure it out, but like all things I couldn't figure out, I didn't dwell on it, but let myself be happy that there was one less person in the world to be making trouble for us. My only worry was that the old bastard's suicide would mean Aaron and Seth would return to be with their mother, and Aaron might come after me again. But I needn't have worried because when they buried the reverend a few days later, we heard that neither Aaron nor Seth had been in attendance. Maybe they were too embarrassed to come. The Christian cemetery would not take him, pastor or no pastor, because he'd died a suicide and he would have to rest—if God let suicides rest and common wisdom held he did not— in the unhallowed ground next to the cemetery where Galen buried its indigents and others without bonafides.

If I'd had any feeling for the reverend's widow, Gale, I might have felt sorry for her. People paid their respects at the funeral, at least most people did, but then everybody in Galen pretty much shunned her. People don't much like being around widows, especially not new widows, because in their hearts they believe widowhood is contagious. And all people avoid the grieving as they can, lest something inside them be similarly stirred to grieving. At least, that's what I've observed.

I didn't have much time to brood on all this though because it seemed no sooner was the reverend in the ground than preparations began for the Christmas dance, the very same dance to which Caroline would accompany Luca. As it happened, a boy named Tom had asked Jolene; so the four of them were going together. Caroline wore blue—to match her eyes, of course, because she believed the secret to a well-lived life was to match one's eyes with one's clothing as much as possible. Jolene's dress was white. I wasn't the best seamstress in the world, but I'd cut the patterns and sewn the seams, and between me and Jewel, we hadn't done a bad job of it. The girls looked pretty, and as we stood on the porch and waved goodbye, I felt proud and proprietary. We watched them walk all the way up the road, until it turned, and we couldn't see them anymore. Then we went back inside, and I made coffee, while Jewel rolled herself a cigarette. The Camels had come to taste bland to her and she had taken to blending her own tobacco. I thought the smell of tobacco foul, but at least Jewel didn't chew, like most men, women, and children in Galen.

"Sit a minute, Darcy," she said to me. "We haven't talked together for the longest time."

"What's on your mind?" I put a cup of coffee, thick as mud, just the way she liked it before her. "Things aren't so bad," I told her, assuming she wanted to talk business. "Four rooms are let. The guy who rode in on a horse drinks, but he pays; the couple in the back room fight, but never after nine o'clock. So I suppose—"

"I don't want to know if the inn is all right. I want to know if *you* are all right."

I considered this question pointless, which was why I never asked it and didn't consider it worth answering. If I wasn't all right, there would be nothing Jewel could do about it, and if Jewel wasn't all right, there would be nothing I could do about it. So why inquire? I waved her away. "Fine, fine, right as rain."

She sighed. "Yes, I guess you are. People like you always come out all right in the end."

Jewel was trying to sound deep and philosophical and it annoyed me. "What do you mean, 'people like me'?"

Jewel always got nervous when she thought she was being pinned down for an answer and she shifted in her chair, clearly hoping that would redirect the conversation. "I don't know quite what I mean."

"That's not unusual."

Jewel leaned forward earnestly. "Wait. I do know what I mean. You were never like Jolene and Caroline as a baby, Darcy. You never let me hold you or comfort you. Even when you were little and you fell down and hurt yourself, you'd go off like an old cur dog to lick your wounds..." *Or to find a place to die like a deer*, I thought. "...And I knew that things would never come easy for you, that everything would be a struggle. And yet no matter how scared I felt for you, I always had the feeling that in the end, somehow, you'd be able to walk away, and everything would be all right. I don't know. Maybe if I'd known who your father was—"

"Oh, please," I said, disgusted. "You're not going to start that again. What difference could it make now?" I'd long since lost whatever curiosity I'd had about my paternity.

"A lot of difference maybe. I should have lied to you. I should have said that your father died but he loved you very much."

"I'd have known you were lying. You can't lie, at least not in a way that anybody would believe."

"I guess you're right," she admitted. "And it's not because I don't want to lie about some things or that I'm above lying. I just don't know how to do it right. That's why it's a good thing you talked to the sheriff that day instead of me. I'd have spilled the beans about Jesse for sure if—"

"You promised never to talk about that again."

"I know I did," she said gently. "But life's going to be very lonely for you if you never tell anyone what you're thinking, or what makes you happy, or the things that keep you awake at night."

Old Sam came in then and put his head in my lap to have his ears scratched.

"What are you thinking, Darcy?" Jewel persisted. "What goes through your mind when you're sitting out on the porch stroking that old dog?"

"Nothing."

"You must be thinking something when you're so quiet like that."

"I'm not Jolene," I snapped. "I don't think about things twenty-four hours in a day just to give my brain exercise."

"Are you thinking that life's been unfair making your sister shine so in school when you're not even going to graduate? Are you thinking how come is it that boys flock to Caroline when you've never even been asked?"

"No."

"Then what are you thinking?"

I looked up at her. "I was thinking that Old Sam's got a big blood-gorged tick in his ear and I should pull it out now before it falls off on the furniture." I rose up in my chair to do just that. "You're always thinking I'm thinking something lofty and important and you're always disappointed to know I just think ordinary things."

"You've got qualities too, Darcy, even if they're not as obvious as your sisters'. You know that you've always been my favorite. God knows, I love your sisters, but you're special."

I laughed a little. "What a wily piece of baggage you are, Jewel Willickers. I've heard you tell the very same thing to Caroline and Jolene at different times when you thought I couldn't hear."

"Well, every child should believe she's her mother's favorite. But with you, Darcy, I really mean it."

I raised an eyebrow. "It's no use."

"Trouble with you, Darcy, is you see things too direct. Sometimes you need to soften the edges a bit. That's why clever people are never cheerful. They see everything at angles."

"Nonsense. Jolene's the smart one."

"I said 'clever,' not smart. And poor Jolene's so smart, she's dumb. And Caroline? I can only wonder what'll come of her. She's plenty in demand now. Why wouldn't she be? Underneath that face is nothing but clay, just waiting to be told what form to take. What man could resist that opportunity? It's like Pyg… that Greek man. But afterwards, when she marries, as girls like her always do, what then? What happens when her husband finds out that instead of a wife, all he's got is an ornament to hang on his Christmas tree?"

"Are you saying I'm lucky to have been born with qualities that aren't as obvious?" I asked sarcastically. I can't deny that I enjoyed seeing her get herself into knots of deception and then try to wriggle out of them.

"Did I hurt you when I said that, Darcy? I didn't mean to."

"Nothing hurts me," I answered.

"How could it when nothing touches you?"

It wasn't really a question and so it didn't require an answer and after a while, Jewel fell asleep with a cigarette still burning in the ashtray. I woke her up to tell her to go to bed before she lit the house on fire.

I stayed awake to wait up for the girls, wanting to get another look at their dresses and moreover to admire my own handiwork. It was after midnight when they came home, and Caroline burst in the door crying. Her dress was all muddy, like she'd been rolling around in dirt. Luca's vest was torn, and blood streaked his white shirt front. "What the—?"

"Luca got in a fight," Caroline blurted out, collapsing into a chair, while Jolene calmly said goodnight to her date and kissed him dispassionately on the cheek. Jolene never upset herself over things that did not directly affect her. Luca muttered foreign words I figured were curses. Blood trickled from his nose and I went into the kitchen to get a towel, wondering how Mr. Popularity could wind up a bloodied mess. I pressed the towel to his face, but he pushed me away. It was clear that his beautiful nose was broken and wasn't ever going to be perfectly straight again. I knew I'd never get a good report from Luca, so I left him to bleed on the carpet and went to Caroline.

"What happened?" I demanded. "I could take a strap to you for getting your dress dirty after all my sewing."

"Oh, Darcy, it was awful," Caroline began. "When Aaron punched Luca in the nose, he fell into me and I fell into a big puddle."

"Aaron?" I felt the blood leave my face. "Aaron Hamilton?"

"None other. Turns out he wasn't away. He came back a while ago and was hiding at home, not going to school or seeing anybody. They say he's the one who found his father swinging from the roof. And tonight— Oh, Darcy, I told Luca to stay out of it."

"Stay out of what?"

She swallowed hard. "You know Clary, the millworker's daughter?"

"Some."

"Well, before he took off, Aaron and her were keeping company. She's loose and wild. Everybody knows that, and she's certainly not worth getting in a fight over." She paused to give Luca a poisonous look. "We were coming out of the dance and we heard somebody yelling at Clary. She was crying and I told Luca we should move on and mind our own business.

But Luca had to be a newsy Esther and he hung back to hear what they were fighting about. Well, it was Aaron and he was all liquored up, calling Clary a whore, and if you ask me, he's right. Then he smacked her across the face with the back of his hand, and that's when Luca stepped in and swung at him." She gave him another poisonous look. "Missed him by a mile and Aaron swung back and knocked Luca unconscious. It took us five minutes to revive him, and by that time, Aaron and Clary were gone."

Hearing Caroline repeat what had happened, and now knowing nobody'd died, I laughed out loud. Luca was a comic sight to behold. All afternoon, he'd been preening in front of the mirror admiring himself. But even as I laughed, I was afraid for him. He was foreign and too naive to appreciate the enemy he had made that night, an enemy who would be exquisitely patient, and all the more dangerous for it. I was afraid for myself, too, given the circumstances in which I'd last seen Aaron. But this was my big chance to torture Luca, and I wasn't about to let it slip away.

"If you'd only minded your own damn business, like Caroline told you, none of this would have happened, you know. Now I might be willing to go everywhere with you and protect you—for a fee. A pantywaist like yourself needs—"

Luca glared at me, eyes burning with all the passion of insulted manhood, and for once I shut up.

We didn't speak to each other for a week after that, and might never have spoken another word to each other ever again, if not for Luca's getting so sick and almost dying on us.

At first, I thought his coming down with measles was hysterical, it being a little kid's disease. But when his fever started to climb and he became delirious, I started to get scared that he really might die. As far as could be told, he had not come from hearty stock—his father having dropped dead without much provocation. What if Luca up and followed suit? I worried. That possibility kept me vigilant and sometimes, when he was too quiet, I'd stick a hand mirror under his nose to make sure he was still breathing.

No one was allowed in the sick room but me. The girls had had the chicken pox but not measles, and Jewel and I couldn't remember if she'd had them or not. I had never had measles or chicken pox or anything else but my strange imperviousness to any kind of illness was just one more of my virtues that wasn't obvious, so I nursed him by myself. That was the way I wanted it. I couldn't have stood for anyone else to take care of him.

Often, when he was out of his head with fever, he would call for his dead mother. It made me uncomfortable to hear a boy nearly full grown to a man calling, "Mama, Mama!" just like a child, and I squirmed whenever I heard it and was embarrassed for him.

Maybe he thought I was his mother because once he reached out and grabbed ahold of my skirt. At first, I tried to shake him off, but it seemed to calm him to have ahold of it, and when I'd satisfied myself that he truly was out of his head, I let his hand stay and didn't even flinch when his arms reached out to encircle my waist. I was never sure how, but sometimes my own arms reached out to touch his hair. It was nice hair, dark and thick as rope. Then my fingers strayed down to his neck. His skin was warm to my touch, warm with fever, and smooth and golden. The sun had tanned him, and the color had not faded with fall. I felt my own skin grow warmer, felt the blood in my face come to the surface. It was a strange sensation for me, and I wondered if I could possibly be getting measles too.

It was then he started rambling again and I wished he could be delirious in English so I could understand. What was he thinking in his feverish brain? Certainly not of me. Of Caroline maybe. Or Jolene or Cathleen Haddock. But never of me.

His long black lashes cast shadows on his cheekbones. The hard work he had done around the inn had left his shoulders broad and his arms heavily muscled. I stared at the veins in his forearms, thinking how vulnerable a man could look when you focused on his veins.

In sleep, his lips were slightly parted, revealing very white teeth. I stared at his hands, long-fingered and fine. Mine were calloused, the nails broken, and the knuckles knobby. It seemed that something was changing between us as he slept and I kept watch over him, but I had no frame of reference then to reason what it could possibly be.

On a morning days later, he was strangely still, with none of the earlier thrashing and moaning. The delirium had left him, and I was afraid that life was going with it. Looking down at him, hoping for a sign, I was taken aback when his eyes opened suddenly.

He smiled weakly, dark circles rimming his eyes, the bones of his face more prominent for the weight he'd lost, and when he spoke, his words were labored. "You are worried," he whispered.

I turned my back to him quickly, dunking a cloth in the basin by the bureau. "So you're back," I said, returning to his bedside to slap the cool rag on his forehead.

"Why are you worried, Darcy? Were you afraid that I would die?" he said with a bashful kind of sweetness.

"Sure, I was. Do you think I wanted to have to go to the expense of burying you? Having to help with your father's funeral was bad enough."

His eyes closed, so I didn't have to turn away this time. There was no need. Things were back to the way they had been before. "Don't go back to sleep just yet. I've got to wash you first."

"Wash me?" His eyes widened.

"Yessir. I've been washing you all week."

The expression on his face told me that it was the first time he realized that underneath the covers, he was naked. He drew the sheet up over his bare chest.

"Oh, don't be silly. I've seen every inch of you, and I didn't find anything unusual."

He clutched the sheet, and as if to turn the tables on me, he began to look at my chest. "Why don't you or the girls wear—the thing?" He drew his hand across his own chest to show what he meant.

"You mean binders?" I asked bluntly. He nodded. "Jewel doesn't believe in binders. She says they keep you from breathing right. Now go back to sleep. I'll just sit here and read my book." I opened my *Rubaiyat* and pretended to read.

He was quiet for a long time after that and I thought he'd fallen back asleep. But then in the middle of the verse, *And this I know: whether the one true light, kindle to love, or wrath consume me quite*, his voice broke into my thoughts.

"Where will you go when you go away, Darcy?" he asked.

I put the book down and looked at him. His eyes were on the ceiling. "Lots of places."

"Where first?" he persisted.

"Are you just asking so as you can laugh at me and get me back for laughing at you?"

"No," he said. "I am not like you. When I ask, it is only because I want to know."

"All right then. Kathmandu. That's where I want to go first."

"Yes, Kathmandu," he said, as if it was familiar to him. "The capital city of Nepal, population: two hundred thousand; form of government: a kingdom, with Hinduism and Buddhism the major religions; climate: from tropical to Arctic, depending on altitude; currency: the rupee, with one hundred paisas in a rupee; language: Nepali, with English taught in some schools…"

I was dumbfounded, but not for long. Soon my amazement turned to anger. Why, somehow, he'd snuck into my room that I kept locked at all times and read my *K* volume of the Encyclopedia. "Where'd you find out all that?" I demanded.

He folded his hands behind his head and continued to stare at the ceiling. "I looked it up in school."

"But why?"

He hesitated. "The first day I came here, you asked me if Italy was near Kathmandu."

I waited. "Well? What reason is that?"

He started to speak, then closed his mouth again. "Maybe someday you will go to Italy," he said finally.

"What would I want to go there for?"

"To see the Colosseum perhaps."

"I don't want to look at old buildings. We got plenty of old buildings right here in Galen."

"Or the Vatican."

"I'm not one of those Catholics. I never even met one."

"The Sistine Chapel."

"The what chapel?"

He breathed a defeated sigh. "It is very beautiful there. That is all I can say." His eyes left the ceiling and moved past me to the window. "That was the good thing about being sick. I dreamed I was home again in Italy. It was so real to me. I wish it was real and not just a dream," he said wistfully.

And it was this very wistfulness that made me suddenly furious with him. "Well, if you want to go back so much, why don't you? Nobody's begging you to stay, and nobody'll remember you two days after you're gone."

"Perhaps that's true," he said. "I would not have spoken of it at all, but I kept picturing you there. It really is the most beautiful country in the world."

"Oh, horseshit! Everybody thinks that about the place where they were born."

He looked at me pointedly. "And do you think that about Galen?"

"Oh, shut up and rest. Else you'll get sick again and I'll be forever nursing you."

After that, his recovery was quick, so that he was able to help with preparations for my surprise party.

I had known about my surprise eighteenth birthday party for some time, and I thought it was the most ridiculous thing that Jewel had thought up to date. And since my birthday was on Halloween, I had the sneaking suspicion they were going to make double fools of themselves by dressing up in costume.

Even now, so many years after, my eighteenth birthday stands out clearly in my memory. It was one of those increasingly rare mornings when I went to school. After school was out, I took a walk so as to give them time to get everything ready, and while

I walked, I practiced my look of surprise that I would put on the moment I stepped through the door. Surprise is not an easy thing to pretend, and much harder than pretending to be mad or sad. I tried raising my eyebrows, but that felt unnatural. I tried jumping a little, but that looked practiced. So I decided on some more subtle gestures.

It had always been my habit to take long solitary walks in the autumn, usually at the time the sun was almost gone and its leaving turned the sky to dirty pink and navy blue. A flock of geese cut a dark triangle across the muted sky and for a few minutes their cries drowned out all other sounds.

The leaves blew up in the wind and circled around my ankles. It would be dark soon, but not just yet. I felt sad all of a sudden. Or not sad, but melancholy, which is a sweeter kind of sadness, and in a perverse way, enjoyable. Maybe it was the days growing shorter that brought on the feeling because when the days got shorter, it always followed that the nights got longer, and it's not easy to shake the feeling that terrible things are about to happen when night begins to last forever. Or maybe it was just that I was never able to lose sight of my own mortality that made me so strange to people and even to myself.

I started across a pumpkin patch, remembering how I'd often crossed the very same patch as a child. I loved the season as much now as I had then, but I had been more joyful when I was young. I used to dive into leaves and kick them up and build houses out of them, and I thought nothing of the dirt that coated them or the bugs that lived beneath them. I suppose it's a sign of maturity to start thinking about dirt. I remembered, too, a time when I would drop my chewing gum on the ground and just pick it up and put it right back into my mouth and not think a thing about it. But after you're five or so, you start to think about it. Dirt and death.

After the pumpkin patch, a field of tall grass lay between me and the inn, and I started out across it. The moon was up already but waning, and not giving much light. Trees lined the field, leafless trees that looked like gnarled old women, which can give you the creeps if you let it. A moment later, I found out firsthand just what surprise looks like. You don't raise your eyebrows or jump up in the air. What you do is freeze into perfect stillness, just as I did when Aaron Hamilton jumped out at me from behind a nearby tree.

I knew it was Aaron right away, even though he was wearing a Halloween mask. Many a time in the past four years, I had felt his eyes on me. Before tonight, I'd always thought it my imagination. But as Jewel had early on observed, I had no imagination, and so all those times, Aaron must have been following me and watching me when I couldn't see him.

He yelled "Boo!"

Instinctively, I backed away, raising my arm to reveal the knife I had taken to carrying. My hand shook visibly as I held the blade high. If only he wasn't wearing the mask, I thought. Seeing his face, I'd read it and know what to do, whether to fight or flee, hold my ground or surrender it.

"Whatta' you pulling a knife on me for?" he asked, sounding genuinely perplexed.

"Get away from me." I brandished the knife at him. "I almost killed you once. This time, I'll really do it."

"Hell, you were just a kid then and didn't know what you was doing," said Aaron generously. "But now you're a full-grown woman."

"And you're a full-grown pig."

He laughed and began to circle me like an Indian. I spun on my heels, knife still raised, so as he shouldn't get behind me. "You shouldn't be calling me names, Miss Willickers. I mean it ain't like you were one of the pretty girls. They got a right to say what they want and get away with it. But somebody plain as you can't afford to pass up no opportunity. It might not come again."

"I'll take the chance."

He lifted his mask, and I got some of my nerve back. His face was quizzical. "You know it's a funny thing, Darcy," he said. "You're not good-looking and you're not sweet-tempered.

But there's something about you. I wish I could say just what. Something that makes a man think you might be worth his while after all."

I jabbed the knife out blindly and hearing him yell, "Shit!" I knew I'd nicked him. He stopped dancing around me long enough to study his arm. The cut couldn't have been too bad because his good humor came quickly back.

He smiled. "I want you to know, Darcy, that I ain't going to hold tonight against you. Just remember, I got nothing but time. And one of these nights, you're going to turn around and there I'll be. Might as well face up to it. You're never going to get away." And with those words, he turned on his heels and was gone.

Shaken, my mind so preoccupied with these new fears, it truly came as a surprise to have Jewel and Luca and the girls dash out from behind the furniture. Sure enough, they had their costumes on. Jolene was a witch with a pointed hat. Caroline was a fairy princess, a part in which she often cast herself even when it wasn't Halloween. Jewel, naturally, was a gypsy, and Luca was a pirate with a scarf tied around his head and a patch over one eye. Jewel plunked a party hat on my head, snapped the elastic under my chin, and I suffered them all to kiss me, except Luca who shook my hand instead.

I felt dazed, but nobody seemed to notice. It would have been a relief to tell them what had happened. To see the fear in their faces would have lessened my own. But that was impossible. They were in a party mood and rowdy as a lynch mob. So I kept it to myself and reasoned that there wasn't really anything they could do about Aaron anyhow. He was as much a fact of life in Galen as the mines.

Out came the birthday cake, a lopsided thing, the result of great effort from Jewel and my sisters. They put eighteen candles on the cake and one for luck, and I made a wish. I put so much thought into my wish that by the time I blew out the candles, they had melted all over the cake. My wish took so long because it was really four wishes in one. I wished that Luca would move out, that Jewel would marry, that the girls would go away to college, and last and most important, that I could then begin my travels, safe in the knowledge that everybody had been provided for and would make no further demands of me.

Naturally, they all wanted to know what I wished, and I said I wished I would travel a lot. Jewel commented that nobody in Galen ever went much of anywhere, and Caroline snickered. Jolene gave me one of her snooty I'm-so-smart looks and told me to cut the cake. Eating that cake, I thought that Jewel was as equally unsuited for the baking profession as for the hospitality profession. If not for the melted wax, the cake wouldn't have had any taste at all.

After we had all choked down the cake, it was time for me to open my presents. Jewel handed me a box from herself and the girls that I could tell came from the dry goods store because of the way it was wrapped, but also because the dry goods store, excepting the general store, was the only store in Galen, which cut down the guesswork considerably. It turned out to be a saw I had admired one day when we'd gone in for supplies. I thanked them politely and wondered why Luca was beaming from ear to ear and looking as expectant as a lady nine-months pregnant.

He stepped aside and I saw a big parcel all wrapped in brown paper. He pushed it toward me and said bashfully, "For you."

Jewel looked at the package. "I'm kind of curious myself. Luca didn't want to go in with us on the saw and he's been so secretive lately."

I had some trouble undoing the string which increased the suspense. Luca looked about to burst and I got suspicious. Maybe it was some kind of prank. So I unwrapped it real careful in case there was a mouse trap or something alive inside there. Slowly, slowly, I let the string fall, and when the paper fell away, I stood back, expecting something to jump out or spring up or go off or whatever. But when I looked, I saw that it was just a suitcase, a plain brown cardboard suitcase. I stood there like a deaf mute and stared at it. From the corner of my eye, I could see Luca beside me, his face full of anticipation, waiting for my reaction.

I looked at him and swallowed hard. I could feel my bottom lip starting to quiver and I bit it to make it stop. I looked up at him again and then back down so that my hair covered my face. The silence was terrible as they waited, sensing something wrong, unable to tell what, looking back and forth from me to each other. I had to think of something to say, something that would put everyone at ease, something witty like Jolene would have done, or maybe the kind of fetching smile that belonged to Caroline. Anything. But I didn't. I didn't because I knew that should I try to speak, my voice would catch and that catch would betray me.

I didn't cry in front of them. That I would never do. Old Sam was the only one who had ever seen me cry, and then not often. So I waited until I had pushed my way past them and was alone and safe in my room. The last thing I heard was Luca's bewildered voice asking, "Didn't she like my present?"

His present. I wondered if he had any idea of just what he had given me. Probably, he believed it was nothing more than a suitcase. How stupid he was and how little he knew about himself or me to think his gift could be just that. It couldn't, not after the time we had talked about Kathmandu. Such a simple message that cheap cardboard suitcase carried and yet it was one that had pierced me to the heart. Did he know? He didn't. Couldn't, as he could not know for I would never tell him that for years afterward, whenever I was feeling certain that everything ended in nothing, I would take out that suitcase that was destined to see virtually no travel in its lifetime, and looking at it, I would feel my heart rise. It hurts to be understood if it's the first time ever. It cracks open the shell of your bitterness and your seeds spill out.

I cried the whole night and yelled at Jewel to go away when she knocked and asked, "Are you all right?" I said I was. But I lied. I wasn't. I never would be again. I buried my face in my pillow and cried without knowing why. I had never been more miserable in my life. And yet there was no more reason to be sad than to be happy. I felt simply split apart, my vitals exposed, as if the very deepest part of me had been opened and could never be sealed up again. Yet I had to find a way to seal it up if I was ever to leave my room and go downstairs. Life, up until that time, had always seemed to me a senseless progression of incidents and coincidence. Things could seldom be arranged and never controlled. But there was one thing of which I was certain in the uncertain world, and that was my own strength. I had never gotten so angry as to forfeit an opportunity, never so relaxed as to let slip a secret, and though I cared for Jewel and the girls, it was never with the blind caring that could divert me from the most practical course. But Luca had cracked the foundation of my bitterness, and if that crack should widen, the whole structure would come tumbling down. I must seal it back up, even if it cost me the thing I held most dear.

I don't need to tell you that things were never the same between me and him after that. I couldn't act natural around him anymore, and so I avoided him. For his part, Luca couldn't understand what he'd done to offend me, because no matter how he tried, I would not be drawn out.

It was the kind of situation Jewel would have thrilled to pick apart at length. There was nothing she enjoyed more than endlessly pondering the motivation behind every deed. For me, that was a waste of time. People did what they did for whatever reason or no reason at all. The end remained the same. Even my own actions, I never stopped to question.

So it followed that I never questioned why I suddenly took to watching Luca when he didn't know it. I watched him across the dinner table. He had impeccable table manners and never made crumbs. I watched him from the shadows of the porch while he flirted with Caroline. He had a courtly way about him that made you feel as if he were just about to ask you to dance. I particularly liked to watch him while he did chores around the house. Sometimes, when chopping wood, he'd take his shirt off. Sweat glistened on every muscle of his broad back and arms.

Never once did he catch me looking, though he tried, turning around suddenly when he must have felt my eyes on him. But I was always too quick for him and by the time he looked up, my eyes had gone back to my fishing line, my sewing, or my reading.

There's no denying that a part of me wanted him to stay with us so I could go on stealing glimpses of him. But a bigger part never stopped wishing he'd get out of our lives, which he had unnecessarily complicated, and go back to Italy. We would all have avoided so much misery. In the spring, he would graduate, and I awaited with great anticipation the fast-approaching day when they would hand him his diploma and he would buy his boat ticket.

Three weeks before the graduation ceremonies were to take place, Luca got into a fight with Mrs. Hennessey over her cat, Emily. It seemed that some animal had gotten mad at Emily—which wasn't surprising, Emily being as old and mean as her mistress—and bitten off a hunk of Emily's ear. It sounded to me like the work of a raccoon. Mrs. Hennessey, for no reason other than that she hated our guts, concluded that Old Sam had done the damage; she marched over to order Luca to shoot the dog for viciousness.

The idea of Old Sam being the guilty one was ridiculous. He was Jewel's dog in disposition and outlook and there wasn't a creature living that Old Sam didn't like. He never chased squirrels like other dogs, and as for cats, why he and Emily had always been friends. Back when Emily was a young mother, Old Sam had been over there every day, just sitting by the basket out on Mrs. Hennessey's front porch, looking down so proud at those kittens, you'd have thought he was the father. Besides that, Old Sam would even let stray male dogs come into his yard—his *own* front yard, mind you—and lift their legs on his very own trees without so much as a bark of protest, and after they were gone, he never ran up behind and wet over the spots where they had wet like most dogs would do. He just sniffed a little to see who the visitor was and left their scent undisturbed on territory that was rightfully his. And he never bothered humans either, not even Mrs. Hennessey when she took a broom to him. Yet this was the dog that she wanted shot.

I was upstairs when she stormed over with broom in hand, and hearing the commotion, I hung out a window to listen and was just in time to hear Luca ask her if she had ridden her broom over or if she had walked. Then in his own formal way, he told her that he would sooner shoot a meddlesome neighbor than he would a harmless dog and finished by telling her never to darken our door again. He'd never shown such spunk before, and in spite of myself, I had to smile. In fact, it was all I could do to keep from applauding. Unfortunately, Luca was soon made to pay for giving the old lady what for, and I was made to pay with him.

A week later, we were paid a visit by the immigration authorities. Someone, who the officials refused to name, had reported Luca as being in this country against the law, and if he didn't leave of his own free will, he would be sent back to Italy.

What a golden opportunity for him, I thought. Here was his chance to get the government of the United States to pay for his return to the country that had spawned him. So you can imagine my surprise when he pleaded with Jewel not to let them send him away.

"You can't be serious," I said to him. "What about all those times you were so homesick? What about Italy being the most beautiful place in the world?"

He didn't argue with me, just sat there with his head in his hands looking miserable.

"Don't you understand anything, Darcy?" Jewel turned on me. "Luca's life is here now. All his friends are here and we're here. We're his family now."

"But he's Eye-talian," I insisted. "And Eye-talian people should be with other Eye-talian people."

She paid me no attention and as I watched her face, I saw an idea take hold. She rose so suddenly that she gave all of us a start, including Luca, who by now was savvy enough to know there was good reason for fear when an idea presented itself to Jewel.

"I know!" she said, and we all shuddered in unison. "We'll marry Luca off to an American girl. They could never deport him if he was the legal husband of a legal United States citizen."

I saw that the wheels were turning a mile a minute in that mind of hers, but never in my wildest imaginings could I have foreseen what came next. With unusual innocence, I said, "Now why would anybody in her right mind agree to marry Luca? He doesn't have a pot to piss in! Who could possibly—" The hairs on the back of my neck stood up as one by one, Jewel, Caroline, Jolene, and finally Luca himself turned to stare at me.

"Wait a minute. If you think… Why should… I won't!"

When the voice of reason came, it was strange to hear it come from Jewel. "Now there's no need to get yourself in a lather. This would purely be a business agreement, and with your mind being so finely attuned to profit and loss, you should certainly be able to digest that." She crossed the room and pushed me into a chair. "Now just sit and hear me out. Luca needs an American wife so he can stay here."

"And the very last thing that I need," I came right back at her, "is a husband to keep me here, and an illegal one at that! Besides, why can't Caroline or Jolene do it? They like him at least."

"Well, isn't that obvious?" Jewel said. "How could we hope to marry them off to rich college boys if they've already got a husband at home?"

"Then marry him yourself." I started to get up, but she pushed me back.

"I shall never marry," she proclaimed, drawing herself up to her full five-foot height. "It's a matter of principle."

I didn't bother to question the reasoning behind that statement. "Well, what about that little tart, Cathleen? She likes anything that shaves."

"She might lift her skirt for anything that shaves," Jolene spoke up knowledgeably. "But she doesn't marry it."

"Cathleen won't have me," Luca said dismally, and from the way he said it, I knew he'd already asked.

"I don't know why you're making such a big deal of it," Jewel said. "All you got to do is marry him and then wait a while and get a divorce and go on with your lives. You're both young. A year or two wasted on a marriage of convenience isn't so bad."

"Convenient for whom, I'd like to know."

Jewel puckered her lips to consider the situation further. "I suppose, in all fairness, there should be some kind of fee paid."

"Oh, I couldn't accept pay from Darcy," Luca said.

"Not her, Luca dear. I meant that you should pay Darcy something for her trouble."

Cautiously, I turned to him. "How much would you be willing to pay?"

He hesitated. "I don't know. Fifty dollars."

"Piss on that amount. I wouldn't even kiss him for fifty dollars."

Before he could come back at me, Jewel stepped in. "It is a bit on the low side, Luca, honey." She turned back to me. "Of course, before we dicker any further, I think we should decide if the marriage is to be consummated."

Luca's cheeks went red. I made a face at her. "If that means will I sleep with him, the answer is no, no, a thousand times no, not for a million dollars."

My emphasis did not impress Jewel. "Then how about three hundred dollars? Three hundred dollars for one unconsummated marriage. Do you think you could raise that to pay Darcy if we gave you enough time?"

Luca nodded miserably.

"And how about you?" Jewel gestured in my direction. "Since the warm glow of having helped another human being isn't enough to satisfy your miserly nature, would three hundred dollars do it?"

"No!" I had just been on the point of considering it, but I knew what miserly meant and I resented being called names. It wasn't miserly to want to own your own life—not other people's lives, mind you, but just your own. Everybody owes themselves that much. Marrying Luca would mean I'd have to put off travel and adventure indefinitely, and even though it might also provide me with the money I'd need to get to Kathmandu, it still seemed one hell of a sacrifice.

"I bet I know what would sweeten the pot," Jewel said, looking at me shrewdly. "What if I was to pay for your honeymoon and send you both away to the seashore for a whole week?"

She had my interest now, if not my cooperation.

"You've never seen the ocean," she reminded me, as if I needed to be reminded. "Luca and you could go up to Wildwood, New Jersey. I've heard about it. They got the ocean and a promenade. And you could stay in a hotel and everything. Wouldn't that be something, Darcy? Staying in a hotel and getting waited on instead of doing the waiting on?"

"Where are you going to get the money to pay for it?" I wanted to know.

She looked down her nose at me. "I don't gotta tell you everything about my personal financial affairs. Never you mind where I'll get it, I'll get it. Is it a deal?"

But there was one thing left for me to find out. "Who's going to pay for the divorce?"

"Luca will," answered his negotiator.

"All right," I conceded. "But only on the condition that he starts saving for the divorce just as soon as we're married."

And that was how I came to marry Luca D'Angeli, partly for the money, and partly for the chance to travel and to finally use my cardboard suitcase that I'd gotten for my birthday.

We stood in front of the justice of the peace. Neither one of us had bothered to wear our good clothes, and Luca promised to love me, and honor me, and all that other manure, and I promised the same. And as we stood there, trying for the justice's benefit, not to act as if the situation were wholly repugnant, I looked into Luca's eyes for the first time in months, and I saw something that made me happy even as it terrified me. But the moment passed too quickly for the truth of what we were doing to penetrate, and he was as much a stranger to me on that day as he had been on the first day, peering out from behind his father. You see, I did not recognize him. Still I did not recognize him.

4

Kindle to Love or Wrath

When the ceremony was over, we got on a train that would take us to Philadelphia and from there to Wildwood. My entire wardrobe, consisting of two pairs of pants without holes in them, and one dress that did not fit me (its rightful owner being Caroline, whose body was different from mine, to say the least) was packed into my suitcase, which I kept on my lap for the whole long ride to New Jersey. I was afraid that someone might steal it, and even at the end of the ride when the conductor offered to take it down the steps for me, I wouldn't let him because I was afraid he'd scratch it. Luca said I should let it get scratched because that was the mark of an experienced traveler and only someone who had never been anywhere would have unscratched luggage, but I wanted it whole and unmarred just the same.

We checked into the Flamingo Hotel, and I thought that if Jewel and I had to be in the hospitality profession, I wished we could have had a hotel like the Flamingo. It was all spanking new with three flamingos in front of the wide veranda. And it was within walking distance of the Boardwalk, being only two miles away. The clerk behind the desk had a nice uniform, which got me thinking that maybe Jewel and I should have been wearing uniforms all these years. He asked if we wanted one room or two.

"One," said Luca.

"Two," said I.

"Adjoining?" the clerk asked.

"On different floors," I answered.

And so we settled into our respective honeymoon suites, me on the first floor, Luca on the second. It was, after all, the only decent thing for two people who were already planning their divorce to do.

My first view of the ocean took my breath away. I'd never been to the sea before. The only bodies of water I had ever seen were the creek that ran not far from the Hospitality Inn and the black waters of the old quarry. So I just stood leaning against the railing of the wooden promenade and stared and stared out to sea. All that water stretching God knew how far around the world. I sighed real deep, thinking how vast it was, when Luca said something to spoil the mood entirely, which was his way. "You should see the Bay of Naples," he said, and if we hadn't been on our honeymoon, I'd have cuffed him then and there. As it was, I just turned away from the view he'd spoiled and started down the boardwalk. He hurried after me and we didn't talk for some time. But I was too happy at being on a trip to stay mad, and soon we were talking again.

There are so many games of chance on the promenade in Wildwood that if you spent the whole day counting them, you'd never count them all. And the prizes. Wonderful prizes. Stuffed animals of every shape and size. Cigarettes if you liked to smoke. Goldfish. Beer glasses. And I wanted to win one of everything.

We played the wheel one time, the one where you put your money on a number and if the arrow stops on it, you win. But I didn't like that game so much. What control had you over where that wheel stopped? None at all. Now if I'd been able to stop that spinning arrow or at least slow it down to better my chances, it would have been a different story. But I didn't trust fate, which had never been kind to me, and so we moved on.

They had a game that was like basketball, only the rim of the basket was narrower than a real basket and they put it up higher and the basket had more bounce than a real one, all of which made it harder to get the ball in the basket. We watched for a while, but we didn't see anybody walk away with a prize. Luca tried, but he missed by a mile. He said it wasn't his game. And so my second chance to win a prize was lost.

Finally we entered an arcade that had all kinds of games to challenge the mind and the body. There was a game where you rolled a hard ball down a narrow alley to four circular holes. If the ball dropped into the largest circle, it was worth ten points, the next largest twenty points, the next largest, thirty, and the smallest, fifty. At this game, you didn't win a prize right off. Instead, you called the boy over and he gave you tickets that were worth one point. We accumulated a lot of points that night. From that game, we went to play another where you rolled small rubber balls into holes that made a section of board light up. It was like playing poker except with balls. But this, too, was a game of luck and not skill, and I had no more faith in luck than I did in fate. Then we found a game Luca was good at—shooting at paper ducks—and we won a lot of points.

By the time they were ready to close, we had twenty-three points in all. We surveyed the prizes: a small dismembered foot that Luca took a shine to; punks to keep the mosquitoes away; eyeglasses without lenses in a variety of colors; rubber spiders; oversized cigars; and a soapy solution to blow bubbles.

We settled upon the eyeglasses without lenses in red for me, and the blow bubble solution for Luca, which I let him get only after he insisted that it was his honeymoon too. We took our prizes out of the arcade, me wearing my eyeglasses and him blowing bubbles down the promenade, just like any other newly married couple out for a summer night's walk in Wildwood.

We walked a long way that night, passed kids our own age, but I didn't see much else we might have had in common with them, passed drunken convention men, prostitutes looking for work, old people resting on pavilion benches, and babies being pushed in buggies. We ate candy and ice cream and didn't throw up. Maybe it was my eyeglasses, or the ice cream, or the salty air, but whatever it was, I was in high spirits that night, and happier than I'd been in a long time. That is, until a conversation

I overheard brought the truth shockingly home and ruined my sham of a honeymoon.

We had stopped to sit on a bench under the pavilion, in front of two young girls. They had stared unabashedly at Luca as we walked the aisle, seeking an empty seat, with an admiration they troubled not at all to hide. Maybe they thought plain looks and bad hearing went together, but as they sat behind us, giggling and whispering, a few remarks came through clearly.

"Isn't he handsome?" one said.

"Did you see his blue eyes?"

"And the dimples when he smiled?"

Hearing them, I smiled too. Obviously, they were talking about Luca, my husband—in name only, but still.

"—I wonder how he got stuck with her.,"

"No wonder she wears glasses."

"But you can still see her face—"

Halfway down the promenade, Luca caught up with me.

"What's wrong?" he asked, breathlessly.

"Nothing," I answered, wondering if he'd heard the girls' snide comments and felt sorry for me. "I just want to go back."

On the way back to the hotel, the fog that had been hovering all night thickened so that it was hard to see, and we walked very close together without touching. Glancing toward him, Luca's profile unnerved me in its perfection, and I wanted to hurt him as badly as I had been hurt. Then it occurred to me that I could simply stop walking. In the fog, he did not notice that I was no longer beside him.

Soon, he did notice, and his voice was casual at first. "Darcy, are you there?" I stood listening. He called again, more fearful this time. "Darcy, where are you?" Then with bravado, "Come out right now! I don't want to play games." And finally, almost appealingly, "Darcy, please come out if you're there."

But I wasn't there, not really. Not then. Not yet. Here was the true test. Here he was, a stranger in a strange place. At night and in a fog, an elemental test, a test of my own design. Did he need me? Would he be able to find his way back without me?

It was a silly way to be thinking, silly and feminine, and I was ashamed of myself. But I did it anyway.

I waited. Soon he gave up looking for me, and I heard him walk away down the boards. Then I, too, started back. Walking alone, I was a little scared myself, but not of getting lost. I trusted my instincts to guide me and when the time came, I would know whether to turn right or left. I was afraid of something much stranger, a thing as murky as the night around me. A kind of struggle between us that had been there from the first day we'd met. Who was stronger? Who was smarter? Who needed who most? And nonsensically, I decided the outcome would be determined by who would be able to find their way back to the hotel first. If it was me, I would be magnanimous in victory. But if he got there first, it would be clear that he did not need me or want me at all, and I would shut him out of my heart as punishment.

I went down the hall to my room with a feeling of terrible suspense. The atmosphere of the hotel that I had earlier admired now seemed only dank and sinister, like the gathering of ill omens. I turned the corner in the hallway and there he sat, leaning against my door.

"What happened to you?" He stood and came to me. "I was afraid you'd gotten lost."

"I don't know," I said crossly. "I guess I lost you in the fog." I took out my key and set it in the lock.

"Aren't you going to ask me in?"

"No. I'm tired and I want to go to bed." I could have left it at that, but some lingering nastiness was yet unsatisfied. "Why would I even think of letting you stay in my room tonight? It's not like we were really married." A bitter taste filled my mouth, as if I'd been chewing tobacco.

"But we are married, or at least we could be if… A husband has a right to—"

"Right, piss! You have no rights. You only married me so as not to get deported."

I watched his face, waiting for him to argue with me. He

seemed to be struggling with what to say next. In the end, neither of us was willing to be at a disadvantage.

He looked around, disoriented. "Well…why did you marry me?"

I looked into his face again for something I did not find, and with great perverse pleasure, I answered, "You know very well why. I did it for three hundred dollars, and you had just better start saving up for that divorce like you promised or I'll get a lawyer myself to notify Italy that I'm returning you." Then I turned around and walked into my room. But it was Luca who would have the last word. I felt heavy hands on my shoulders turning me around roughly to face him, his face close enough that I could feel his breath on my cheek. His eyes filled my vision, a field of blue as big as the sea. But not their usual shade. Hot blue, warmed with something akin to hate.

"I don't think I'm getting my money's worth," he said and left, slamming the door as he went.

I didn't see him again until it was time to get the train back and what Luca did with the time left to him on our honeymoon is unknown to this day.

A lot can happen in a couple of years, or almost nothing at all. And during the two years after we had come back from Wildwood, nothing happened that stands out in my mind. We ate, drank, slept, and grew older, with nothing much to make one day different from the next.

One thing though. I remember being driven half crazy by a key I found one day in the pocket of an old dress I hadn't worn for years. It was a key like any other, and I tried that key in the front door, the back door, my bedroom door, and even the door of the truck that seldom ran and sat collecting rust out front of the house. It got me to thinking of Leon, the truck's original owner, and I wondered if he were still alive and what he was doing if he were alive, or really what he was doing if he wasn't alive for that matter. *There was a door to which I found no key.*

There was a veil past which I could not see. Some little talk awhile of me and thee there seemed—and then no more of thee and me. It was in the natural order of things to have a lock and lose the key and quite out of the order of things to find the key and lose the lock. That was just like with Luca and me. By the time I found I loved him, I had nearly lost him for all time.

Maybe I had known it all along and maybe that was the reason I'd despised him right off. Maybe he had known it, too, and dreading it, had reconciled himself, nevertheless. That would be like him, always facing up to things no matter how terrible. And how terrible the prospect of marrying me must have been. How he must have shuddered to think of it, for surely, I was not what he'd hoped for in his schoolboy dreams.

Pretty people should marry other pretty people. It's better for everybody that way, and Luca should have married Caroline, or someone else as pretty as himself. Still, I was shortchanging him. For all his beauty, his aristocratic nose, clear blue eyes, and perfectly aligned teeth, Luca was not a Caroline. There was more to him than that.

I hadn't wanted to notice anything nice about Luca before. I'd been too busy thinking up ways to torture him and put as great a distance as possible between us. How very successful I had been. It was too late now to call to him. He would be too far away ever to hear me again. All this, I'd done by myself, and I took a twisted pride in having been able to ruin things so thoroughly without any help. Now, we hardly ever spoke at all. Yet in the widening silence, I saw for the first time how it really was with him.

He'd been a proud boy who had grown into a proud man, but one who had been forced to swallow that pride so often that it had choked off something inside him. Humility did not become him, and I could not stand to see him humbled. It was like seeing royalty dethroned, or a mountain lion made docile. He should have been cocky and conceited. He should have been bold and unafraid. But he was none of those things. When Luca raised a fork to eat, his hands shook, and I knew that something at the core of him was shaking too, its foundation soon to rent asunder.

There was one thing more I found out about Luca in those days of silence, and that was that he cared for me. Not loved. He did not love me. But he cared for me, and believing I had no right to expect more, it would have been enough, if I had not known the reasons for his care. It was in Luca's nature to always take the part of the weak, the homely, the outcast. And while I didn't mind him thinking me homely and outcast, I couldn't bear knowing that at some time, when I was unaware, he had seen me weak, and moved by the sight, had come to care for me. I could stand to be hated, taunted, shunned, but not this, this terrible compassion.

Luca. I can hardly stand to tell of him during those two years. He changed so much that it was as if we hardly knew him. While I blamed myself for the change, it was the mines, I knew, that really did him in.

After we came back from New Jersey, Luca started working in the mines, the only work he could find, despite knowing five languages. There was no demand for linguists in Galen.

Jewel begged him not to do it. She said it wasn't natural for men to work in dark little holes in the ground. She said it would break his back and his spirit and he'd be old before his time. She said that with his cleverness and knowledge of five languages, he should be a diplomat or an ambassador or something important. She begged me to talk to him. She said that working in the mines would keep him from ever reaching his potential. But I knew it was useless, and all I could say was, "How many of us will reach our potential, Jewel? Will I? Did you?"

All of us noticed the change in him. I can't remember him ever smiling in those years, so that everybody almost forgot what nice teeth and dimples he had. Except me. I never forgot how he looked when he smiled, and I watched and waited but I wouldn't see it again for a long time. He seldom spoke to me, and even when he did, it was never a word more than necessary. He didn't talk much to Caroline or Jolene either, and when they talked, he seemed to begrudge them an answer. Only with Jewel, he never changed. Only with her was he unfailingly patient and kind.

Every week he insisted on turning his pay over to her, and I wondered how he could be saving for our divorce if he gave all his money away like that. But I never got the chance to ask him, because we were never alone together, and I sensed that that was as he wanted it. Every night, he'd come home all full of soot and coughing up dust, and after he'd wash up, Jewel would serve him dinner, and after he'd finish, he would go to bed or fall asleep over his coffee.

He never complained. Not once. Not ever. But it must have been bitter to him all the same. He'd come here looking for opportunity and instead had found coal. It was what he woke to and what he dreamed about at night. Not the coal exactly, but the tunnels. Jewel was the only one he talked to about it. I heard him tell her once that he had nightmares about the tunnel collapsing on him and being buried alive. He told her how every day he felt certain that the space had gotten smaller, and how he felt always nauseous and got persistent headaches even when he wasn't in the mine. Still, he would always add, it wasn't really so bad as it sounded and he didn't truly mind it so much.

When the whole business of living got too much for me, I always thought of Kathmandu and watching his brooding face, I wondered what it was he thought of when things went badly. Probably escaping us all and going back to Italy. I knew nothing of his country, and yet I feared its power. Always there was the threat that someday it would call him back home again, and he would go. Luca never talked about Italy anymore and that was maybe most disturbing of all because it was like he had forgotten all the things that had once made him happy and now all that was left was a creature that worked and ate and slept and woke to do it again the next morning. Nothing more.

Jewel was changing, too, in a different way. She was getting thinner and thinner, and soon her shapely form that had been such a joy to the boys in Texas began to look almost childlike with its flat chest and narrow hips. Sometimes she had trouble breathing and I'd scold her not to smoke so much. But she'd always tell me to mind my own business.

In September of the next year, we sent the girls off to college. It wasn't a real good school but it was the one we managed to afford. Before the girls left, I sat them down for a long talk to remind them what the whole purpose of their going away to college was for: To meet and marry rich husbands, and that they had better devote themselves to the task at hand and never let studying get in the way of the main goal. Caroline, I knew, would obey me, partly because she was easily cowed and partly because stalking potential husbands came so naturally to her. But with my youngest sister, I was less confident, for like Jewel, Jolene was the kind who would hang on your every word, nodding agreement after every sentence, never saying anything to contradict you, and then go ahead and do exactly what she pleased and to hell with you. So it was anyone's guess how Jolene would end up.

After the girls were gone, the house got so quiet that it made me want to scream, what with Jewel grown unusually silent, and Luca always too tired to make much noise. Maybe it was the awful stillness that started my sleeplessness.

There's nothing worse than not being able to sleep, than lying awake staring into the dark, convinced that every other living soul on God's good earth was asleep and that you, and you alone out of all mankind, were still wide awake while the rest of humanity peacefully slumbered. Luca had told me once that in Italy time runs ahead, so that when it's midnight here, it's almost morning there, and I got some comfort imagining all those Eye-talians running around starting breakfast. But dammit to hell, this was not Italy and it was not morning in my bedroom, but the heart of the night, and if I did not fall asleep soon, I would jump off the roof and hang myself as the reverend had done.

Of course, getting mad only revived me more. So then I tried clearing my mind of all thoughts, which if you've ever tried it, you know is impossible. My mind stayed clear for about three seconds before who should pop into it but Cathleen Haddock, Luca's old crush. I hadn't seen her since my rare visits to high school, but now against my will, I remembered her in detail. What a shame that she and Luca had never married. She was just his type. Pert and pretty, with a petite figure and pleasing personality, and agreeable as the day was long. Cathleen had married some boy from West Virginia, and when Caroline had told Luca about it, I'd watched his face but he hadn't even blinked. Of course, that was an act. He just didn't want to give me the satisfaction of seeing how smitten he truly was and what a terrible blow her wedding another was to him.

From there my thoughts went on to wondering if Cathleen's marriage was what had started Luca visiting the whorehouse in the woods every Tuesday and Thursday nights. I supposed he was too tired for some things but not for others. And since tonight was Tuesday and well after midnight, I didn't have to wonder with what my lawfully wedded husband was occupied.

Soon, I quit trying to sleep and went downstairs to sit on the porch. I wasn't afraid to sit out in the dark alone. The only one who might have been lurking about was Aaron and he had enlisted in the Army the year before to avoid the mines. It was very hot out, in spite of it being September, and I didn't bother to put on a wrapper. My nightgown was enough and no one would see me in the dark anyway. The gown had belonged to Jewel, old but still pretty, of pale blue satin with lace over the bust. Jewel had worn it as a girl, but since losing so much weight, it kept falling off her shoulders and she'd given it to me.

Putting it on for the first time, I was amazed how well I filled it out. My chest and hips were as full and round as Jewel's had always been until a few months before. Remembering a picture I'd seen of her, it crossed my mind that I was built rather like her except bigger. But the thought passed quickly and never for a moment in a self-congratulatory way. If I ever thought about my body at all, it was only when it wasn't working right. If I couldn't lift something, I'd wish my back was stronger; or if I couldn't haul something, I'd wish my legs had more muscle. I never wondered if my arms and legs and hips and chest, and the way they came together, were pleasing to the eye. But as I sat in the rocking chair with my legs tucked up under me and Old Sam in his customary place beneath my chair, I wondered exactly that.

I leaned back in the shadows and listened to Old Sam snore. Until my untimely rising, he'd been asleep at the foot of my bed, but when I got up, so did he. That's the wonderful thing about dogs. When you want to sleep, they sleep with you, and if you should want to get up, even if it's one o'clock in the morning, they get up with you and follow wherever you like, even into Hades, judging from Old Sam. Thinking of his congeniality, I reached down to rub his ears. He was getting old now and not as alert as he'd been as a pup. So he didn't even stir when Luca came up the stairs, making them creak.

From the recesses of the porch, I watched him in the moonlight. He looked haggard but not dirty, and it piqued me to know that wherever he'd been he'd taken off his clothes and had a bath. He didn't notice me, and I could have let him pass unseeing, but it had been so long since he'd directed a word at me, even a hateful one, that I thought even mean words would be better than none at all.

"Through whoring for the evening, I see." It was an observation sure to get the conversation started.

He gave a start, but if I'd hoped to arouse him, I was soon disappointed. He turned to me with tired eyes, and said simply, "It's none of your business where I spend my nights or who I spend them with."

His tiredness made me even angrier than knowing he'd taken a bath somewhere naked, and I said, "Listen, you foreign bastard!" So suddenly did I come to my feet that Old Sam was jolted awake and ran off howling. "You married me for your own rotten selfish reasons, and now you went off and made a fool of me with whores and sluts and all kinds of lowlife."

"We had an agreement—" he began wearily.

"You're damn right we had an agreement! You agreed to save up for a divorce and so far, I haven't seen one red cent for divorce money. Now just when do you plan on getting that divorce you promised?" I stood before him with hands on hips, glad that I was tall enough to stare him down.

"Soon," he answered with a reassurance that enraged me. "I'm tired and I'm going to bed."

"Oh no, you're not, damn you," I said, blocking his path. "You used me and took advantage of me, and you married me just because Jolene and Caroline and Cathleen wouldn't have you, and now you're going to stay right there until I've finished telling you just what I think of you. Why are you looking at me like that?" I was put off by the way his gaze kept travelling up and down the length of me.

He gave me a half smile. "I was thinking that the next time you decide to play innocence wronged, you should choose a more appropriate costume."

For the first time in my tirade, I was aware of the thin lace over the breast of the blue satin nightgown that Jewel had originally bought to thrill the justice. I was embarrassed. Hoping now to abandon the conversation and that he would continue on his way upstairs, I shrunk back into the darkest corner of the porch. But he did not leave, and his face seemed to change as he slowly came toward me, his lips parted but not in a smile, his eyes holding mine. My back touched the porch rail, preventing further retreat.

"And now you will listen to me," he spoke with authority, in a voice that was at once soft and rough, like a cat's tongue. "And you will not interrupt. The day I came here to the inn, yours was the first face I saw. Shy, I hid behind my father, but I was watching you all the time. You came around front, wiping your bloody hands on an apron. How fascinated I was with this girl with the bloodied hands. And then your sisters came out, too, and I looked at Caroline and saw how beautiful she was with her black hair and blue eyes. But when I looked from her to you, I was confused. The one is very beautiful, I thought. The other, less so. But what is it about the girl with bloody hands that makes the other seem so ordinary?"

My knees buckled a little because I was falling under the spell of his soft eyes, the lullaby in his voice, a voice ever-tinged with the music of the language he had first spoken. He touched my arm lightly, and even that slight touch seared down to my bones, so that I felt it in the core of me, something shifting and melting.

"…And later, after I had lived here a while, I was drawn to you. But I was just a boy and the things that a man wants are not the desires of a boy. I was still a child and I wanted dolls to play with. So I pursued the doll and hoped that you would wait for me to grow up…"

He brushed a strand of hair from my forehead and then his fingers, calloused from his work, dropped to my chin and he turned my head up toward him so that I felt his breath on my face.

"…And when I married you, I did it for selfish reasons, yes, but not for those you think. It's true I wouldn't have married you if I hadn't had to. Still a boy, I was not fit to marry anyone. But if I had to marry, I was happy that it was you. I knew that given time, I would come to love you. I always wanted you—yes, *wanted*, Darcy. Don't pull away from me. Wanted to feel myself inside you, to feel your warmth around me, to see your face change when you felt me for the first time…"

I could feel my face turning red like a fool but still I could not bring myself to turn away. The hand that held my chin was gentle but unyielding.

"…But it was more than that. I admired you and looked up to you as someone who had something to teach me. You seemed to have seen so much of life, and I was willing to learn from you. There was so much inside here." He touched my breast over my heart. "Your courage, your strength, your loyalty, your ambition, not just for yourself, but even more for those you love. Even your brutality. Yes, even that I admired. And so I knew that you were meant for me, and that I would love you, almost from the beginning, because I wanted you and admired you, and when there is desire and respect, love is never far behind…"

Time passed or must have, and it seemed to have left us in its wake. I was enchanted as in a fairy story, kissed by fate and time, and in my trance, there was nothing but whispered words, and warm skin and gentle hands.

Then into the dream came a sensation both strange and familiar. The hands were no longer gentle but possessed of something I remembered vaguely from a long ago nightmare. They reached under the lace of Jewel's nightgown, purposeful and rough. His mouth was against my throat and I couldn't turn my head. I smelled whiskey on him. Pinned against the side of the porch, I strained against him and felt him rock hard against me, his whole body grown taut and driving. His breath came fast and shallow as he pressed into me, again and again, rhythmically, in a violent dance that demanded more than I could give just at that moment. I felt his teeth in my shoulder, and it hurt. Most hurtful of all was that he seemed so unaware of me, as if it might have been anyone or anything against him, and he would be pleased, so long as it was soft and warm. Like that day with Aaron. Not just like it, but like it enough to make me panic, to make me forget the porch and remember the barn, remember the feeling of heedless hands grabbing at my clothes. There'd been a sickle to grab then. There wasn't one now. But ever resourceful, I was always my own best weapon.

My knee came up between his legs and at the same time I pushed him away from me hard.

"I hate you," I said, as he doubled up against the wall. "You ruined my life and I hate you." I tried to sound cold and dignified but my breath came too quickly.

As I moved around him, he straightened up and grabbed me, but not like before. This time, there was no passion in his grasp, and just enough force to prevent me from passing.

"You don't hate me," he said, "though you'd like to. You don't want me to touch you and you don't want me to touch anyone else. You'd like to keep me in a jar where you could look at me once in a while with the lid tightly closed." And with that, he let me go.

Running upstairs, I caught Jewel's nightgown on a nail and tore it. In the safety of my locked room, I took it off and got under the sheets naked. My teeth chattered, though the room was hot, and at the same time, I felt the sheets beneath me dampening with sweat as I took the pillow and covered my head with it. Sometime, near dawn, I fell asleep and when I woke, the only clear thing to me was that nothing was clear to me. The world and all its creatures were an abiding mystery, and nowhere dwelled a more mysterious creature than I to myself. It seemed to me that hate is a tortured kind of love, but that didn't make sense at all.

Downstairs, Jewel sat alone at the breakfast table. "Luca didn't come down to breakfast this morning," she said. "He left a note that he'd put in for a double shift and not to wait up for him."

I listened to her talk and realized that Luca had won after all. Last night, I had locked my door against him. This morning, he had locked his heart against me forever. And I might have grieved in my own way over this, were it not that soon, as in every life, new troubles came to take the place of the old.

5

Like Snow Upon the Desert's Dusty Face

I guess I have no medical aptitude. All along I'd thought Jewel had a bad heart because of the trouble she had breathing sometimes and the sudden pains that made her wince. But it wasn't her heart at all.

I could almost feel sorry for the young doctor who told us that Jewel's lungs were being eaten away with disease and that there wasn't a whole lot they could do for her. He seemed embarrassed, like it was his fault.

Jewel didn't even blink when he told us. She listened politely when he suggested we take a room close to the clinic where they could at least try to do something for her, and she nodded and said that it was an excellent idea. Then the doctor reminded her that she must stop smoking at once, and Jewel wholeheartedly agreed. But that young doctor didn't know Jewel, and not knowing her, he believed what she said. I knew better.

As soon as we were clear of the clinic, Jewel lit herself up a smoke. "Don't you believe a word those doctors say, Darcy. They always exaggerate so as they can charge more. All I've got is bronchitis, and it'll pass just like it always has. Now swear to God you won't say anything about it to the girls." Reluctantly, I swore. "They might be sympathetic and the worst thing for the sick is sympathy. Makes a person that much sicker because they've got to be worthy of it."

Caroline came home that summer engaged. She had really come through for us this time. Her betrothed was a freshly graduated lawyer who would be joining his father's practice in Connecticut. Of course, he had not gone to the same school as Caroline, which wouldn't have been nearly good enough for him, but a prestigious one in his home state. (*Prestigious* was the first word Caroline had ever mastered that was more than two syllables, and she managed to use it at least fifty times during the first week she was home.) Caroline had met her lawyer at a tennis match, when his prestigious school had condescended to play Caroline's. He sounded like a sissy to me, but he was a monied sissy, and Caroline, who never could look out for herself, would need somebody with money. Caroline would be leaving college as soon as they married. There was no point to it anymore.

Results with Jolene were less satisfactory, but I could have predicted that. She had chosen to attend classes straight through the summer. Journalism was her major, and Caroline, a natural tattletale if ever there was one, told us that Jolene was sleeping regularly with her married journalism professor. My youngest sister was nobody's fool though. The professor had promised her a job working for a friend of his on a newspaper in New York as soon as she graduated. Jolene wanted to be a foreign correspondent and go all over the world corresponding. I wondered if she would ever get to go to Kathmandu and the possibility made me heartsick.

Originally, Caroline and the lawyer had planned to get married the following spring. But Jewel, who never did trust too-long engagements, convinced them to do it in the fall. Luca agreed. He said, "Macaroni and matrimony have to go fast." I guess it was some Eye-talian saying.

After the wedding, which we didn't attend because Jewel wasn't well enough, Caroline moved into a big new house in Connecticut. We never did get to see it, but she sent us pictures of every angle and view.

For a girl who wanted to be a correspondent, Jolene hardly ever wrote home. She came back to Galen exactly twice during her stretch at college, and I could have slapped her face the first time she returned, acting so bored with us all, as if we were morons in comparison to her college friends. The second time she came back, it wasn't to see us at all but to cover a story for her school newspaper. It's hard to believe something newsworthy could happen in Galen, but it did. Naturally, it was a disaster story, and Jewel and I were some of the first to know about it.

On a February night, as we sat close to the fire because we couldn't afford heat that year, somebody started banging at the door, and just from the way they banged, you knew the person on the other end had nothing good to tell. A man stood on the threshold carrying a lantern that turned his face yellow. He wasted no words.

"You got a foreign boy staying here with you?"

"Yes."

"Well, he's one of them. Been an accident at the mine. You better come."

Jewel came with me even though I wanted her to stay home. The cold could only make her condition worse. But since she never believed she had a condition, she didn't believe that anything could make it worse. Made me wonder if after she died, she would believe she was dead, and if she didn't believe she was dead, would that make her a ghost?

The collapsed shaft didn't look any different to me. The entrance hadn't been damaged, but one of the tunnels inside had fallen in. A lot of men were running around yelling orders to each other while a small group of women huddled together against the cold. Unwillingly, I followed Jewel to stand with them. It was like standing in a graveyard. Not one of them spoke, not even to each other, and they were too scared even to be snooty to us. A child clung to the skirt of one girl and she neither picked him up nor pushed him away. I don't think she realized he was there. Every eye was fixed on the mine. An old woman who could stand no longer, sat down on the frozen ground, and rubbed her bony hands together.

By and by, one of the hurrying men must have noticed how wretched the women looked because he came over and lit a fire in a metal can. But the women didn't notice the man or the fire and not a one went over to warm herself.

There was something that set Jewel apart from the other women, and I suppose it was surprise. She was surprised that such a thing could happen. They were not. They had been expecting disaster all their lives, and this was my only link with them.

"Why don't you go home? You can't do anything here," I said, when I saw Jewel's lips were blue.

She shivered but otherwise didn't move. "You can't do anything either, but I don't see you going."

"Well, there's no reason for both of us to be here."

"Then you go home," she said stubbornly. "I'm staying until they bring him out alive or.... Either way, I'm staying."

The whole night passed like that. The cold, the mute women, the urgent men. Toward daylight, they brought out one of them, and the women surged forward and scanned the blackened face. No one had to tell them he was dead. His head tilted at an impossible angle, his eyes unnaturally half open, slits of white against the black. He didn't look at all like Luca, and so I was spared that moment when you think it just might be someone who belongs to you. The corpse was the son of the old woman. She came forward to wipe his face just to make sure, a few seconds of false hope. Then a single deep shudder, but not a tear. Maybe she'd lost others like this. She was old enough to have lost a husband or a brother. Accidents were not rare. Or maybe she'd wait to get home to cry. Whatever, she walked away ramrod straight.

Somebody started a soup pot and I got some for Jewel, whose face was by now as ashen as her cigarette butts. I knew it was useless to tell her to go home. All her life, she had seemed to give in, but I know, looking back, that she had never given an inch.

Two of the rescuers had to quit because of frostbite, but there were others to take the places of those who looked as dead as the dead man.

Soon some newspaper people started coming and we were really taken aback to see Jolene come up beside us. She had been chosen to write about the accident because Galen was her hometown. Jolene never could stand to be uncomfortable and she lasted about forty-five minutes before she went back to the inn. "I'll interview the survivors," she said in a sprightly way, "if there are any."

A few hours later, they reached the place where the four remaining men were trapped. One by one, they were carried out, the first with a blanket over his head. It was not Luca. Luca was the last to be taken out, and when I saw it was him, I felt my heart stop, just like when you sneeze. He was so still, so still. I took his cold, limp hand and pressed it to my mouth, and then I saw something that made my heart rise. Steam. Vapor rising from his nose and mouth in the cold air.

They let me get into the ambulance with him, and I held his hand and whispered to him the whole way. I could say anything I wanted because he couldn't hear. So I told him that I loved him, that I had always, always loved him, long before I had known it myself and that if he would live I would never be mean to him again.

They kept him in the hospital for a week and on the day he was to come home, I was nervous, wondering how I should act around him. I sat by the front window with my *Rubaiyat* in my hand, but I couldn't read. I kept listening to hear him come up the walk.

When I heard his step, I went to the window and parted the curtain and saw him climbing the steps clumsily, with one leg that didn't bend at the knee. He held a cane in one hand. If I craned my neck, I could see his face. He kept blinking and swallowing, and his jaw was working, as if it took courage just to knock.

I didn't wait for his knock. I threw open the door with a gladness too strong to hide. But as he stood before me and I could see him up close for the first time since before the accident, the gladness drained out of me. Without meaning to, I recoiled from the sight of him. It was a stranger at the door, and not the familiar stranger I remembered. Who was this stooped man leaning on his cane, I wondered, and what was this terrible manhood that had settled on his features and made them leaden? How much more had been lost to him than the full use of his leg? My eyes shifted awkwardly. For a split second, I moved to take his arm and then just as suddenly, withdrew it.

"Well, don't just leave him standing there," Jewel said, approaching from behind. "Let him in so I can look at him." She put an arm around him and led him into the parlor. That had always been Jewel's part to play with the guests, to soothe them. Mine was to discomfit them. She looked him up and down appraisingly. "Why, you're fine, and none the worse for wear," she pronounced, but her eyes lingered a moment too long on his leg and even from across the room, I saw him flinch. "Now you just sit down and chat with Darcy, while I go in and see to dinner," she said, as if either one of us had ever been capable of chatter.

Our eyes met for a second before we looked away. I heard him seat himself with difficulty. I'd never thought about it before, but it must be hard to sit down when one leg doesn't bend right. After he'd managed it, he pressed each of the five fingertips of one hand against the tips of the other and studied them. Then he stood up just as awkwardly as he'd sat down and went to poke the fire. After he had poked all the life out of the fire, he sat down again. The room had been quiet for so long that I startled when he said, "How is she, Darcy?"

"Jewel? She's all right," I told him because that was the answer she'd sworn me to give.

"You're not a stupid girl. You know better than that." He shook his head slowly and his voice was grave. "She's very sick. I can see it and so must you."

"What about you?" I said. "Are you all right?"

He seemed unprepared for the question, but he nodded, and while I still had my nerve, I spoke again. "What will you do now that—well, now that you can't work anymore?"

He sighed. "I'll be getting some money from the accident. It'll be enough to live on for a while and when I'm ready, I'll go home."

"Home? I thought this was your home."

"No," he said, in way that made me think he'd given it great thought. "Once, it might have been. Not now."

He looked away from me and continued as if he was directing his words to someone else in the room. "…All I've known here is death and pain and strangeness. I want to go back where there are people who know me, who speak my language and understand me."

"I thought you didn't have any family left in Italy."

"An uncle. A few cousins. But there are others, people who knew my father who will welcome me when I get there. Had you never thought of that, Darcy?"

His voice was even but I could tell that something had made him angry. I didn't answer directly. "Well, don't let me keep you from going home to all those people who are waiting for you with open arms."

He looked at me. "It's not you who keeps me here."

"I never thought it was. Probably one of those tarts in that house in the woods you were always visiting."

"No."

"Then who? Don't keep me in suspense."

"Jewel, obviously. I'd have thought you'd have known, but I forget how insensitive you are about anything other than food or shelter. She's the one I stay for."

"Jewel?"

"She was the only one in Galen who was ever really kind to me. Now that she's dying, I won't leave her. At the end, she may need me." He inclined his head. "I don't see Caroline or Jolene coming back here for anything. And even you may need me at the end— Oh, don't be so quick to refuse. You think you are so strong. And maybe you have been, but it was only because you had her behind you."

"Behind me? Jewel never once—"

"She didn't have to," he anticipated me. "You always knew she was there, whether you called on her or not. And when she's not there anymore, you're going to need someone."

"I wasn't the one who needed a wife to stay in this country. You were. Jewel and me got along fine long before you came and we'll get along fine long after you're gone."

"Just the same," he said, the anger gone out of his voice, "I'll stay until the end...for her."

Then, Jewel called us in to dinner.

It took her months to die, her lungs rotting away slowly in her chest, and even then, when she got back a little of her strength, she'd ask me for a cigarette. I always lit it up for her. It was too late to matter now, but I thought that I had never seen anything more obscene than the sight of her using her last bit of wind to suck on it. Then again, at least she'd never chewed.

Luca went in to see her every day, but he could never force himself to stay for long. He was the kind who could stand pain, but not to watch it. Having to watch it takes a different kind of fortitude. He would always leave her room, white-faced, to go back to his chores. Hard work seemed to purge him somehow, and the exhaustion that followed dragging that bad leg around with him all day, I suppose, gave him some kind of peace.

My conversations with Jewel went down some peculiar byways in those last months and it drove the point home to me how much we are ever to remain strangers to each other on this earth, no matter how close the connection. But some of the mystery that was Mary Margaret Willickers was solved for me. For one thing, I'd always assumed she was the only child of the reverend and his wife simply because she had never talked about any brothers or sisters. Turns out she'd had a brother all right.

"His name was Henry," Jewel told me, "but we called him Joss. He was five years older than me. I adored him. So did my mama before she died, and I guess that was what the reverend had against him. When he was sixteen, he left home and stowed away on a ship for England. There were some of Mama's people still in Cornwall and he wanted to know them. He promised one day he would send for me and we'd be together again. He said he would write to me and I should be sure to meet the postman first because the reverend was sure to tear up the letters if he got his hands on them. He didn't write for a long time and when he did it was to tell me that he'd joined the army with some cousins we had over there. He thought it was going to be a wonderful adventure, going to war. He'd just been in a big battle in Belgium in August, his regiment and a French one. He'd gotten hurt bad and was in a hospital in Paris. But he wasn't really writing to me about that. He wanted me to know about something that had happened to him in case he died. He said that they'd been retreating because they were being slaughtered by the Germans, and being overrun, they didn't see any way out. But that was when they all saw a tall man with yellow hair, covering their retreat. Well, Joss was six feet five inches in bare feet. In fact,when the circus came to town one summer, they'd invited him to go with them. So I couldn't imagine how Joss could be describing anybody as 'tall.' All of humanity was pretty short from his perspective. Joss said the man was riding a white horse and carrying a sword, and crying, 'Victory!' Well, I still didn't think it was that unusual. But when Joss said the man with the yellow hair was about thirty feet tall, I knew something was amiss…"

I stood near her bed, folding clean linens. Though our washing machine hadn't worked for years and all our laundry had to be done by hand with a washboard, I changed her bed sheets every day so as they'd always smell fresh. There was so little else I could do for her now.

"…Well, Joss died a few days later. A nurse from the hospital wrote to tell me. I figured he was out of his mind with fear or pain when he saw that thirty-foot yellow-haired man with the sword on horseback…"

"Of course, he was," I agreed absently. I was used to her saying odd things. The morphine worked on her pain, but it also worked on her mind, and there were times when she thought she was a little girl again in Texas. I never had any trouble picturing her as a child. Rather, I'd always had trouble picturing her as an adult.

"But now I'm not so sure…"

"About what?"

"About the yellow-haired man."

"Why?"

"Because the last couple of days, off and on, there's been a Negro with feathers standing beside my door watching me." Reflexively I looked to the door. "Do you see him?" she asked.

I didn't, of course, and I'd just given her a whopping dose of morphine, but I didn't see the point in arguing with her either. "Yes, I see him," I said agreeably.

"Liar! He's not there now. Funny it should be a Negro. The only Negro I ever really knew was the girl who kept house for us in Texas after Mama died. Her name was Josephina. The reverend never allowed her to speak in his presence. And I don't think I've seen one ever in Galen."

"Why don't you tell him to go away if you don't like him watching you?"

"I do like it. He's here for a reason. Like the song." She began to hum, "…comin' for to carry me home…"

"Stop it!"

"Remember that night, Darcy?"

"What night?" I said, but I knew.

"The night you came home from reform school."

"I don't want to talk about it."

She bunched up the pillows so that she could lean her elbows on them. "We've got to talk about it. And now. Because after I'm gone, there won't be anybody left you can talk about it with. Unless you plan on telling Luca."

"I'd never tell him."

"Why? He'd never tell on us."

"He wouldn't understand. He's like you. He thinks people are better than they are. And he's so disappointed when he finds they're just as rotten as everybody else."

"You're probably best off not telling, I guess. He's too honest for his own good. A lie like that would eat at him. How well do you remember that night?"

"It's not something a person's likely to forget. I mean the body was two days old and getting gamey by the time I got home." I didn't like the turn the conversation had taken, so I took up a pile of socks and tried to match them.

"Where'd you put him, Darcy?"

"In the orchard," I said. I couldn't seem to find the mate to a navy blue one. "There's a spot where the earth was soft. Too soft, maybe. Twice I caught Old Sam sniffing around the spot and once he started digging and I had to chase him away."

"Do you know what happened that night, Darcy?"

She was looking at me sharply now with none of the morphine haze that sometimes dimmed her eyes. I wouldn't look up. "No, and I don't care." It was some years now since Jesse had made his grand entrance into our lives and it felt like a hundred.

"Well, what do you think happened? In all these years, you must have formed some idea."

"I figure you and Jesse had a fight and you killed him. He was such a little turd, it wouldn't have taken much to do him in. Then you panicked and sent a message to me."

She looked suddenly disappointed. "Don't you remember what I told you that night, before you dragged him away?"

"You said, 'I want you to know I didn't do it.'"

"Well, didn't you believe me?"

"No. I did not."

"I'm telling you I didn't do it." She was getting herself all worked up now, and I wished there was a way to stop this talk, but it had been coming on too long.

"Then who did?" I asked flippantly. Maybe I was still holding a grudge. Even now, it galled me to think how I'd had to leave the Schuylkill County School for Wayward Girls in the middle of the night without even a chance to say goodbye to the librarian.

Jewel didn't answer right away, still hurt that I had never believed her. Then she opened her mouth to speak, closed it, opened it again, and said, "Reverend Hamilton did it."

Too shocked to react, I could only let my mouth hang open like an idiot.

"Reverend Hamilton killed Jesse," she repeated.

"How?"

"He pushed him and—"

"I don't mean *how'd* it happen. I mean *why'd* it happen?" I tried and failed not to be angry at a sick woman, but thinking how I'd gone to all that trouble to cover up for a man whose guts I'd always hated was more than I could swallow gracefully.

"It wasn't really his fault," Jewel was quick to say. "He didn't mean to do it. It's just one thing led to another."

"What things?" I asked, tight-lipped.

After a deep sigh, she began. "Me and Jesse were fighting as usual. After you were gone, he got real bossy, tried to make me give him money. But I knew he just wanted money so as he could leave. Oh, stop looking at me like that. I'm not the first woman who ever acted like a fool because she was afraid of being left. Anyway, we were fighting the night Hamilton came and he walked right into the thick of things. Jesse told him to get out, but Hamilton wouldn't go until he'd said what he'd come to say. And oddly, it was you, Darcy, he'd come to talk about."

"Me?"

"Yep. He said maybe he hadn't been fair to you the way he'd acted about Aaron getting cut and all. He said, upon reflection, it was probably more Aaron's doing than yours. Said he'd found out something that made him realize that. He thought maybe you were better off in reform school and away from the inn and Galen, that if you were given a decent upbringing, you'd grow into a fine young woman, and if I was any kind of mother, I'd use the time you were away to rid myself of all the evil influences around the inn, starting with bloodsuckers like Jesse. Well, Jesse took offence at that, naturally, and he said it was you, Darcy, who made all the trouble and that you were just no good, and the best thing for everybody would be if you never came home."

She began coughing then and I went to get her water. After

a few sips, she said, "I couldn't let him say those things about you, my own child, and I turned on him like a snake. I said Reverend Hamilton made sense about getting rid of him, and I wanted him to leave that very night. That was when Jesse went crazy. He smashed every lamp in the room, and the girls came running up to the landing, but I told them to go back to their rooms and not come out again that night, no matter what they heard. Then Jesse grabbed me by the throat, and I thought he was going to break my neck. But the reverend came up and made him let me go. That's when Jesse hit him, which wasn't right because the reverend had twenty years on Jesse. I thought he'd never get up when Jesse knocked him down, but he did. Got up finally and hit Jesse right back. It wasn't a very solid punch, no force to it and poorly aimed. Which is why the reverend and I just kept looking at each other when Jesse didn't come back at him again. Then we saw the blood running out the side of his head, and we knew he'd hit something going down."

She stopped talking then and bowed her head like she was in church, I guess in reverence for the deceased, but I felt no such reverence, and I wanted to hear the rest. "And then what happenened?"

"Everything got very confusing after that. The reverend was so shaken I had to get some liquor into him, and I was in no condition myself to be comforting him. He missed his mouth and spilled liquor all down his shirtfront. 'My God, my God,' he kept saying, 'I've killed a man.'" I didn't say a word because I was almost as scared as him. He said we should get a doctor, but we both knew it was too late for that. Then he came up with the worst idea of all. He wanted to go for the sheriff, and you know how nervous police and clergy make me, and to have both under my roof at the same time would have been more than I could stand. I had to think fast. I told him if it got out, he'd be ruined. And seeing as how he hadn't meant to do it, there was no reason for him to tell anybody. Poor man. He just kept nodding his head up and down like a woodpecker and running his fingers through what hair he had left. 'What shall I do?' he kept repeating. I thought I'd go mad if he said it one more time. So I told him to go home and not say a word to anybody. I'd take care of everything. That's when I sat down and wrote my message to you. I waited for the postman next morning, and I gave him twenty dollars to see to it that my letter got to you right away. I knew you'd know what to do, Darcy. You always know what to do."

I laughed soundlessly. The spit in my mouth tasted of bile. To her death, Jewel would never know quite what to do about anything.

"I'm sorry I sent that letter, Darcy. I ought never to have drug you into it, except that I knew you'd take care of it better than any of us could."

"I'm glad you did," I said. "I can only imagine where we'd all be today if you hadn't. What I can't understand is why you'd risk everything you had for a man who lived to make trouble for us."

She twisted her bed covers in her hand and said, "I can't really explain that even to myself. It just seems like when you try to decide who's bad and who's good, it's too tangled to figure out. I mean if the reverend hadn't wanted to talk about your upbringing and then if he hadn't unwound Jesse's fingers from my throat, none of it would've happened. And Jesse wasn't always a son of a bitch. Sometimes, he'd make me laugh and laugh. But once Jesse was dead, there was nothing I could do for him, but I could help the reverend and he needed help badly. I've done plenty of things I'm ashamed of, but I have never refused a human being my help. And it's always come back to me, the help when I needed it, because the world is round."

What the shape of the world had to do with anything escaped me but I knew that that had been as close to an explanation as Jewel would ever get. So I gave up on that particular line of questioning and instead asked something that had me curious. "Do you suppose Jesse's dying was why the reverend killed himself?"

"It couldn't have helped but I don't think that's the reason. I saw him a couple of months before he hung himself. He sent me a message by way of his housekeeper to meet him out in the orchard. He looked awful that day, pale and sweating. He said, 'I've done terrible things, Jewel. I've killed a man, but I can live with that. What I can't live with is that I've raised a boy who's done worse than killing.' Then he said that I should keep Aaron away from you because there was something about you that stirred up all the evil in him. I took offense at that because it was like he was saying it was your fault. So I said, 'Why don't *you* keep Aaron away from Darcy?' and he said, 'I will as long as I can.' And that was the last I ever saw him alive."

"What could Aaron have done worse than killing?" I wondered aloud.

"I don't know. But killing yourself is just as bad. It's outside the natural order of things and puts a big rent in the universe."

I rolled my eyes, but she didn't seem to notice.

"In a way, I'm to blame for Hamilton's dying. I never wanted to confess. I never needed to. I figured God sees everything you do, and that's enough. But he needed to confess, and I should have let him."

"It's all over with now anyhow."

"Is it? I don't think anything is ever over once it happens. It's just like an echo down a well. What if someone takes a notion to dig up the orchard someday looking for Jesse?"

"You don't ever have to worry about that," I said, unable to keep from smiling at my own cleverness. "Before I buried him, I took off his pants and jacket and I put them on and his helmet too. I'd watched him start his motorcycle a hundred times, so it wasn't hard to figure out. I took it up on the ridge and waited most of the day until I saw Mrs. Hennessey come out. I waved to her from up there with the helmet on, so she couldn't see my face. She didn't wave back naturally, just walked off in a huff, but I knew she'd seen me. She don't miss a trick. I know she told everybody she could about it. She loves to be important and knowing something nobody else did must have given her a little thrill. I left his motorcycle in back of a diner on the highway and pulled out some wires so it wouldn't start. It looked like he'd broke down and maybe got a ride with a trucker. Then I buried his clothes and his helmet and walked back hell for leather through the woods in my slip, hoping nobody saw me. Nobody did. If the body ever does turn up, they'll never know it's his."

Jewel looked at me wordlessly. "You're scarin' me a little bit." She paused again thoughtfully. "You know I wonder sometimes why Aaron's the way he is. I wonder if he was born like that or if something made him that way. Maybe the reverend beat the devil into him while he was trying to beat it out of him. It's like what come first the chicken or the egg."

We stopped talking after that, and as the afternoon turned to evening, I watched Jewel's eyes close and went to pull the sheet up over her shoulders so that she wouldn't catch a chill. She stirred. "Sit by me, Darcy," she said, "just until I fall asleep." I pulled up a chair and felt her take my hand to lay against her cheek. "Such warm, rough hands," she said, and I could feel that she was smiling in the encroaching darkness. "Don't grieve for me when I'm gone."

"I won't," I said. "I'll be too mad to grieve. It's fine for you. Dying doesn't mean anything to you. You don't believe in it. But I believe in it, and when you're gone, I'll be left alone, all by myself, until I get so old, I lose all my teeth and can't chew food. Then I'll starve to death."

She laughed softly. "You're so dramatic. It won't be as bad as all that. You'll still have Luca."

"Like hell, I will. Once you're gone, he'll hop on the first boat back to Italy."

"Then tell him you love him. You do love him, don't you, Darcy?"

I was glad for the dark. I could have never answered otherwise.

"What's the difference? It's all ruined anyhow. I don't blame him. I did it. He could have loved me once. But not anymore."

She laughed again. "All ruined? Just because the puppy dog

love you might have had together is gone, doesn't mean it's all gone. You've got to be grateful for the love that's left. It's ruined love. But it's still love. You still have that. I see it in his eyes when he looks at you."

"I think the morphine is stimulating your imagination. What you think you see in his eyes is as real as that Negro by the door."

"I pity you, Darcy, you know that. You love him from hell to breakfast, but you can't say it and you can't show it. Your love just sticks in your throat like a chicken bone. It must have been torture for him to be around you all these years and never know, and worse for you to be around him all this time and never tell. Why do human beings torment themselves so?"

Old Sam jumped on the bed and curled up at Jewel's feet. He'd never done that before. Usually he'd just lay down at the bedroom threshold, near to where Jewel said the Negro was waiting. I made to push him down, but Jewel said to let him be.

That afternoon was to be the last time I spoke to my mother. My mother. How strange the words sounded to me. Jewel. An innocent right up to the end. A child. A gentle and beautiful child who the world had bloodied but never made bitter. How could she have possibly ever been anyone's mother? But she was, had been, a mother, second to none. A mother who had found the best in each of us, mined it, and never made us feel the lack of what we would never have to give. She was, after all was said and done, my mother, though I never called her anything but Jewel, and the next day, she died in my arms.

It was a glorious day, the first sunny one in what seemed like endless days of rain. Luca was in the orchard tending the trees. I didn't have to tell him. I could see in his face what he had seen in mine, the knowledge that made him lean so heavily on his spade. "It's over," I said. "She's gone."

He didn't say anything, just closed his eyes. Finally, he said, "I'm sorry, Darcy."

And I said, "Thank you," and had started back to the house, when his hand touched my shoulder. "Let me help with the funeral," he said.

"That's all right," I said. "I'd rather do it myself. It'll give me something to do."

His eyes fell back to his spade then, and he went back to his work, and I to the house. It never occurred to me that he might have needed to help me even if I didn't need help, that perhaps he was already missing Jewel as much as I was. It just never occurred to me.

It turned bitter cold the day of the funeral and Caroline showed up looking like something out of a magazine, complete with black-veiled hat and gloves. Over her dress, she wore a fur coat that must have cost her lawyer husband the proceeds of a major lawsuit. Even Jolene breezed in from Philadelphia, where she had won a scholarship to keep going to school.

It was a simple service conducted by a minister Caroline had brought with her from Connecticut over my objections. Jewel had never thought much of churchmen or churchgoers and I didn't think it fitting to have one at the funeral. But Caroline said it wouldn't be proper, and I gave in to her who had developed a mortal fear of being improper. Her husband took us all to the service in his big black car that must have been a mile long. During the service, he kept taking his watch out of his pocket every five seconds and looking at it like he had a train to catch.

The minister talked for a while by the graveside in a very general way since he had never met Jewel, and then we all threw a rose onto the lowered coffin. I watched Luca drop his rose and thought I'd never seen anyone look so stricken. When it was over, I felt disgusted with myself for letting Caroline take over like she had. And I asked if anyone would mind if I read from a book I'd read to Jewel in her last months. It was not really a question and I didn't wait for a response. I just took out my *Rubaiyat*: "*Then said another—surely not in vain my substance from the common earth was ta'en, that He who subtly wrought me into shape should stamp me back to common earth again.*"

The minister had a hissyfit and said it wasn't right to read pagan verse on such an occasion. So for spite, I followed up with: "*Ah, with the grape my fading life provide, and wash my body whence the life has died, and in a windingsheet of vineleaf wrapt, so bury me by some sweet gardenside."*

Walking back to the car, Caroline's husband took her arm and the minister took Jolene's. I hoped Luca might offer me his arm, but he walked by himself a little ahead of the rest of us with his hands in his pockets. And so, I walked alone.

Back at the inn, Jolene left right away. She had to get back for some examinations, she said over her shoulder as she swept out the door. Luca went upstairs to change his good clothes and Caroline and her husband proceeded to ransack the house under the guise of collecting mementos of Jewel.

In every family, there is a vulture, for some unfortunate families more than one, who can smell death even from great distance, and once having caught the scent, cannot rest until all that once belonged to the dead is theirs. Often, they swoop down on the house before the undertaker can get there. Sometimes, they cannot even wait for death, but begin to dismantle the house piece by piece while the sick still live. With a cold eye, they appraise value, and with greedy fingers, they grasp and carry off in their talons whatever isn't nailed to the floor. Caroline was our very own vulture, and in the time she had been gone from Galen, she had developed an appreciation for antiques. To me, the inn and all its contents were junk, but to Caroline's practiced eye, the things that had belonged to the justice and then to Jewel, were valuable. She filled her big black car with small chairs and tables and lamps and jewelry and anything else that could be made to fit. For a moment, I thought she was going to tie her husband to the car roof to make more room for her plunder. She was good enough, however, to leave me my bed and enough skeletal furniture to keep the house functioning.

Luca stood in the hall watching Caroline go in and out with an expression of disgust. I, too, was disgusted and wanted to slap her face and pull her hair, but having so recently put Jewel in the ground, I didn't have the stomach for a brawl. Then, too, when your mother dies, you hear her voice for good or ill for the rest of your life. And I could hear Jewel saying, "Let her have it, Darcy. There's nothing going with her that you'll ever need." So I let her take it all and was glad to hear at last her mile-long car pull away.

The rituals of death had tired me, and I felt very cold. Watching a coffin being lowered into the ground can make you feel cold, even in July. You start to think of the day when it's your turn to get lowered into the cold earth and laid away to eternal darkness. Someone had started a fire in the drawing room. Luca, most likely since it wasn't me, and Caroline and Mr. Caroline probably had servants for that kind of thing. I could smell it, and drawn to the warmth, I went in to find Luca there. He was just pouring himself a glass of brandy.

He looked up and saw me. His eyes had a hard glint. "Join me," he said and got another glass. "We'll have a farewell drink together."

"Farewell?" I made my voice hold nothing more than passing interest. "Are you leaving?"

Laughter rose from low in his throat, and I began to think he had been drinking for a while before I came in. "Come now, Darcy, this can't be a surprise to you. Since the day I arrived, you've wanted me to leave. There were times I thought it was your life's work. Still, I suppose it is surprising. I mean, you bullied and begged, all to no purpose, and now with no effort from you, I'm finally going. It's miraculous." He paused and moved closer. "Stop frowning," he said. "It makes you look old. You never did have a pretty smile. But you always had the most attractive frown. But seriously, Jewel's gone, and that's why I'm leaving. While she lived, I did my best to show my gratitude, even suffering to live with her insufferable daughters. You were all a dose of bitter medicine in your own way, you know. But it's pointless to try to show gratitude to the dead. In a way, Jewel released me from my prison." He motioned around the room and the look he'd worn at the graveside returned fleetingly to his features and was quickly gone. He forced a smile. "But you must not worry. You will do fine alone. After all, you've been preparing for something awful to happen most of your life. Now that it finally has, it must be almost a relief."

"You came to the inn," I said. "That was awful enough."

He laughed again. "Ah, Darcy, Darcy. Most people look on tragedy and think, 'Why me?' You look on tragedy and say, "Why not me?" He raised the glass to his mouth and drank the last of it. "Enough conversation. I'll be gone in the morning."

"Where do you plan on going?"

"Does it matter?" He flashed his dimples at me. "But you're probably thinking of the money I still owe you. Well, you'll be happy to know that I've left enough for you to divorce me. You can tell them I deserted you. That will simplify things." He pointed a finger at me, and his face turned suddenly fierce. "But I won't have you telling anyone that I forced myself on you, even though I could have. Rightfully. You tell them that you're as much a virgin as the day you were born. Do you hear me?"

"Go to hell!"

He was very angry now. "That doesn't mean very much to you, does it, Darcy?" His eyes darkened to navy. "How many men do you think would have let you keep your door locked every night when they were in possession of a legal paper that gave them the right to be in your bed? How wasted gallantry is on someone like you."

"Gallantry, piss! You left me alone because you knew that I could kick your backside from here all the way back to Italy—and because you had whores in that house in the woods."

The smirk hadn't left my face before he was on top of me, his arm around my waist. Dragging me across the room, he pushed me down on the couch. I could feel its old springs digging in my back, as the weight of him made us both sink down into threadbare upholstery. I turned my face away.

"Get off me, you son of a bitch!"

"Look at me!" he said.

"Leave me alone," I answered, my face still averted.

His hand reached up to tangle in my hair, and I winced as his grip tightened, forcing my head around.

"Kiss me, Darcy, kiss me goodbye…" He held my chin.

"Get away from me."

"Are you stronger than me? Answer me. Are you?"

"Yes!" Tears pricked my eyes from the stinging in my scalp. "What—what are you doing?" He was pinning my arms behind my back, using my own weight to confine me. He was stronger than I would have thought. The face of an aristocrat on the body of a laborer. The muscles of his arms strained against the material of his shirt. His legs were muscled, too, though the one maimed in the accident had shriveled somewhat. I felt the muscles of his thighs against my own, and then his knees forcing my legs apart. He loomed over me, unsmiling now, his breath laced with the smell of brandy and coming in great gasps. I could hardly breathe with him pressing into me, and maybe it was this that made me go suddenly limp. It was over. He could do whatever he liked with me. What was there to lose? I had no family left, no sisters, no mother, nothing to struggle for, nothing to hope for. Only the inn. The cold, drafty inn. And some day when a terrible stench arose that the neighbors could no longer ignore, they would enter with handkerchiefs over their noses to remove my dead body. Suddenly, I surrendered to whatever was to be my lot in life.

And just as suddenly, he got up and went and sat across the room, where he lit a cigarette. "Get up," he ordered, and I did. Without his body to cover me, the cold in the room rushed up and gathered around me like mist. I was surprised that I didn't feel embarrassed, only mystified and a little disappointed.

As if to explain himself, he spoke again. "I don't want to hear any more talk of who is stronger. It's childish." He gestured with the cigarette. "I could have done anything I wanted with you a moment ago. But I don't want you that way. I never did." He inhaled on the cigarette. "Let's not argue any more. I'm not waiting till morning. I'll be gone tonight, and I'd much rather leave on good terms."

I smoothed my hair back and asked, "Have you packed yet?"

"No."

"Do you—would you like me to help you?" I was a good packer, despite the fact I'd only packed the one time for our honeymoon. Long ago, I had drawn up a packing list of things I would take with me to Kathmandu, and every so often I revised it. But Luca didn't want me to help.

"It isn't necessary," he said. "I've so few possessions. I hope you don't mind if I take your suitcase. I have none of my own."

"You mean the one you gave me for my birthday?" I asked, amazed at his gall.

"The very one."

"I sure as hell do mind. It was a present and I think it's mighty stingy of you to take it back now. Why can't you put your things in a paper sack?"

"I'd look like a vagrant."

"You'd look like a vagrant anyway with that old suitcase. The cardboard's bubbled and the clasps are rusted."

"Then why do you want to keep it if it's so badly worn?"

"Because…" I began, resenting the need for explanation. "Because it's mine!"

"Very well," he said unmiffed. "There's another bag I found in my closet. Someone must have left it. I'll use that."

"Oh no, you won't."

"Why not? Whoever left it, I'm sure he's not coming back for it after all these years."

"You can't have it because it's official property of the inn."

He laughed out loud. "All right. I will leave the inn and all its contents intact." He made to leave the room, but I blocked his way.

"Why are you rushing off all of a sudden?"

"It's not sudden. I've meant to leave a hundred times before this." He pushed past me.

"Can't you wait just a little while," I persisted, "a few weeks, maybe, just until I get everything straightened out here?"

He turned on the first landing of the stair. "No. The inn has never been straightened out. It never will be."

I tried to think of more to say, but nothing was forthcoming.

So in frustration, I blurted out, "You're a bastard to leave me this way."

He turned and drew himself up, offended. "What insults I've borne today. Earlier, I was the son of a dog and now my parentage is in question. You're not a poor little girl, Darcy, and you're as unconvincing now as you were that night on the porch a few summers ago."

I felt the color come to my face, remembering that night, and I spoke quickly hoping he would not notice. "You were disgusting that night."

He smiled at me. "Then it's just as well I go. If I were to stay in the house with you, I would probably be disgusting again… and again and again."

He was teasing me, but I wasn't up to it. There were more serious things to consider. "What would I have to do to get you to stay for a little while?" I watched as he dimpled all over and showed his perfect teeth. "You're enjoying this, aren't you?"

"I am."

"Well, don't expect me to tell you how wonderful you are. Or to make some dramatic declaration that would only embarrass us both."

"If I had wanted that, I'd have married Caroline."

"She wouldn't have you," I reminded him.

"That's my wife," he said laughing, "Never lets me get too pleased with myself," and then suddenly he wasn't laughing anymore, and there was a new light in his eyes.

On the landing just above me, he reached out. "Come here to me," he said quietly, and I went without any more hesitation in the direction I had slowly and fitfully been moving all along.

"There is only one thing I want for us, Darcy," he whispered into my hair. "I want us to live as husband and wife and to love each other until we are so old that it seems we were born together. We need never talk about it, but we'll know. We'll know it's there beneath all the trouble that will come to us."

I didn't speak. It was just what I wanted to say to him, put into words better than I ever could have. So I just swallowed and nodded and followed him up the stairs with a feeling of ascension that was more than just the simple act of climbing to the second floor.

6

Some Corner of the Hubbub Couch'd

We didn't go to his bedroom. We didn't go to mine. We took the best room at the inn and one we had rarely used except for the most special of guests. And Luca and I, we were special guests, special guests in a special place, known briefly, lost soon, and grieved forever.

Time slowed as I sat on the bed, wishing it were darker so that he could not see my face, but glad of enough light to see his. I watched him take off his shirt. Fascinated, I watched each finger undo each button. There were five of them.

"Take your clothes off," he said, and I started to unbutton my own dress with shaking fingers. Luca had been with so many girls. I knew I could be with only one man ever. I would be awkward, clumsy, and how he would laugh at me then. I had a sinking feeling and wished fervently that I was somewhere else, but not for long, because when I again looked up, he stood before me naked and the beauty of his golden body made me forget everything, even my own nakedness. How silly I must have looked to him, my mouth opened in maidenly awe, my bare arms hanging dumbly onto the bed. What a chance for him to get back at me then, to humiliate me for all the years I had tormented him. But he didn't seem to want to embarrass me. Instead, he just said, "Come to me. I've waited so long," and I felt such love and forgiveness in his voice that I went into his arms naturally and without awkwardness.

The linen sheets were cool and crisp and new. They had never been slept on but awaited some high-paying guest who had never materialized.

"Tell me what to do," I said. It was the first and last time I would ever ask for direction. After that night, I always knew just what to do and how and when.

"Kiss me," he said, and as he did, he kissed me softly, chastely, not like a lover at all, but more like a person at an altar, and this infinite gentleness surprised me.

He kissed my throat and I shivered.

"Are you cold?"

"A little."

"I'll make you warm," he promised, and he did. His mouth went to my breast, and I felt his even teeth, but ever so lightly, and his hands reached down under the sheet to grasp the back of my legs, and he kissed my stomach. His fingertips pressed into my thighs, parting them, and I felt his mouth again and my breath caught.

"Don't—"

"Don't what?" His voice was muffled.

"Don't kiss me there."

"Why?"

"I—I don't like it."

"You don't know it," he said patiently, but ignoring the words, for he knew them for what they were, words of unreasoned shame. "And when you do, you'll want it. You'll want me," he said knowingly. "You'll want me as I want you, everywhere, in every way."

I had no answer to give, so I closed my eyes and waited and that was as it should have been for nothing could have prepared me for what I felt then. A kind of excitement and anticipation so excruciating that I almost wanted to run from it, to escape it and him, because I suddenly felt that if it were to go on like this, then I would die, or be reborn, but born different and strange to myself. By some mysterious process, he was draining my will, drawing it into himself, controlling me as surely as he now controlled my limbs, raising them to bend at the knees, and if I let him, it would be the end of me, the beginning of someone new, but the end of me.

I would not die so easily, would not give myself up to him without a struggle. So I struggled from habit more than will, strained against him and tried to twist away, but he was the stronger, at least that night. I was truly losing myself, and not just to him anymore. But to some dark fathomless force that lay behind all life's beauty and all its mystery, and I began to feel indistinct, my edges blurring, my bones becoming fluid and flowing to the sea, and the bed itself seemed as if it were moving in a series of undulating waves that would drown me if I let it.

"Please, stop—I—" My voice did not sound like my voice. It sounded strangled. But he didn't stop until every muscle tensed inside me, and I held on to him as if he was at once my only link to the world and what most separated me from it.

He held me and stroked my hair and whispered, "It's all right," and I tried to believe him as the room spun around me. The room was very hot now, hot and sweaty and oppressive, as if it was summer instead of fall. I wanted to sleep. Sleep was the thing. I couldn't remember ever having been so tired. Weary, but never like this, not with this feeling of having lost all desire or motivation to move. Always before there had been something, hunger or thirst or the need for amusement, or simply to be left alone. Now I wanted for nothing. Except sleep.

But he wouldn't let me sleep, and as soon as the faintness began to subside, his mouth was on mine again, not gentle now, but with something like violence. Yet his violence was never to frighten me half as much as did his tenderness. The violence, I understood.

"Are you going to—?"

"Yes," he said.

"Now?"

I felt him nod.

"Will it—?"

"A little."

"What if—?"

But there was no time to ask because all at once he was

inside me, the shock of fullness, of sudden wholeness. Unmoving at first, he sighed deeply and then began to move, slowly, then quicker, growing bigger with each thrust, heedless of me, of anything but the moment. The brass headboard of the bed banged against the wall loudly, but he didn't seem to notice, so intent was he on his own motions. Nor did he flinch when I bit his lip and drew a drop of blood that I could taste, unaware of his own pain or of mine, a pain that increased as he grew within me. Surely he would burst me wide open, but it was not me who burst, but him, and I heard him cry my name as he did, like a curse or an appeal to God. He shuddered and held me so tightly that it cut off my breath, and then all at once he went limp against me, as if I'd taken all the life from him into my own body. With his full weight upon me, I could not close my legs, which had begun to cramp. He was still inside me now. Unmoving, but within me, and I did not want him to go. Finally, he rolled off me and onto his back, and I missed him so that he might have gone half a world away, instead of only to the other side of the bed.

I fell asleep soon afterward, too tired to be self-conscious that he was still awake and watching me. It was good to fall asleep first, in the warmth of his gaze. When I woke up, his arm was around me, one leg thrust over mine. I loved him very much that morning because he slept so sweetly, and I felt hopeful and full of the certainty that good things were on the way, because surely nothing could come between us as long as we could sleep wound around each other every night.

It had taken me twenty-three years to get into bed with a man, but I took to it with a shameful lack of shame, mostly because for all my immodesty, I always held something back, something of myself, in case one day I should need it. Luca said that I was brutal, but he meant it as a compliment. So I never took offense. Early on, I stopped wearing a nightgown to bed which disturbed Luca's sense of propriety, and he clung to his pajama bottoms stubbornly, until the day I took scissors to the only pair he owned. Thereafter, he slept naked too and I could touch him all night as much as I liked and feel his warmth against me.

I especially liked to trace the scar that ran from above his thigh to just below his hip. His scar was like a secret we shared, and like all secrets, it somehow bound us together. He had fallen through a window when he was just a boy and had almost bled to death, and it scared me to think that he could have bled to death in Italy and I'd never have known him. Sometimes, I'd trace his scar too lightly, and he'd slap my hand and say, "Stop it, Darcy. You're tickling me." Then I'd trace it harder, and he always knew what that meant. We never had to say much to each other to know when it was time to be together. We were silent then, except for the words Luca would whisper against my throat just before he finished. Foreign words that had no meaning for me, and he would not tell me what they meant. He said if I was going to learn to speak Italian, it just wasn't right to learn those kinds of words first. But I didn't want to learn. It would have made me strange to myself to speak Italian.

In the morning, I liked to watch him shave, and it got to be a ritual. I would sit on the commode tank with my feet on the seat, and he would go through the elaborate procedure of soaping his face with a brush and sharpening his razor with a strop and then making narrow strips from his cheeks to under his chin. My eyes followed every stroke. I don't know why I got so much pleasure out of watching him shave, except that it was probably the same reason that made him like to watch me brush my hair.

We fought a lot, about all sorts of things, and for some reason, at the very point when we were most frenzied and ready to spit on each other, I would begin to want him. And that was how all our fights ended, sweetly and without the need for words. It helped too that Luca had never really lost his accent, so that even when we fought and he wanted to be mean, everything came out sounding like endearments.

Sometimes at night, lying in our bed, when sleep wouldn't come quickly, we would talk. With my head on his shoulder, I'd watch the glow of his cigarette in the dark and tell him things that I had never told another living soul. Luca somehow, in his patient, unhurried way, made me remember things I hadn't thought of in years. He liked to talk about Italy. He had grown up an urchin on the streets of Naples, his mother having died when he was a baby and his father preoccupied with keeping a roof over their heads and food on the table. He hadn't felt particularly motherless because in Naples all the grown-ups raised all the children. When he had turned sixteen, his father wanted a better life for his son and to see him educated. So with the money they had accumulated, they traveled to America. But even more than talking about his life, Luca liked to draw me out about my own experiences growing up in Galen.

"You don't seem to fit in with the rest of the people here," he said to me.

"I never wanted to," I told him.

"You sound like it's a matter of honor not to be like the others."

"It is…to me. But the funny thing is that you fit in here just fine."

"Oh, I can fit in anywhere," he said wistfully. "My father raised me to fit in."

"How's that?"

He sighed. "As a young man, he'd had to leave Naples to find work in Switzerland. That's how the poor people do it in Italy. The men go off for months to wherever there is work. So children grow up without fathers. Speaking only Italian, he was marked as a foreigner. He met a German girl there. He told me about her once. It was long before he met my mother. He wanted to marry the girl, but her father wouldn't allow it. I think my father thought of that girl till the day he died." Luca's voice was filled with regret. "I think he loved that girl more than he ever did my mother. That's why we are so lucky, my Darcy. We got to marry the one we loved. Hardly anybody gets to do that for one reason or another." He kissed me.

"What does the German girl have to do with you fitting in?"

"Well, it was very bitter to my father that he'd been rejected, and he never stopped believing that if he'd spoken German, he would have been able to make a place for himself in Switzerland, and everything would have turned out differently. When I was born, he was determined that I would learn to speak as many languages as my brain would hold. He was willing to go without food to pay for tutors."

I laughed. "The other boys must have made fun of you."

"Yes. They called me *professore.* I told my father how I was suffering but he wasn't sympathetic. He said, 'Your friends are morons and I'm not going to raise you to be a moron just so a bunch of morons will accept you.' He felt that if I knew languages and cultures, I could live anywhere and never be shut out as he was in Switzerland."

"I guess he was right," I offered.

"Right? Maybe. But it was him who loved the German, not me. Why must we always restore to our fathers whatever they missed in life? Why must we undo their mistakes when their mistakes have nothing to do with our mistakes?"

Feeling I had missed the point, I didn't even try to answer. After a while, he whispered, "Darcy, are you asleep?"

"No. It's too hot to sleep. Shall we change position? Has your arm fallen asleep under me?"

"No. Let's stay like this."

"All right."

"In fact, let's not sleep at all," he suggested. "I don't like to sleep. How can I know I'll ever wake again?"

"I wouldn't worry. Most people aren't lucky enough to die in their sleep. Most die at length and in agony…like Jewel." I felt his arm tighten around me.

"You miss her very much, don't you?"

"Yes. But I'm angry too."

"Why?"

"That she lived and died, and it didn't mean a damn thing."

"I don't understand."

"I don't either. It doesn't seem right that she should have been so nice to everybody all her life and then die like that. It came to nothing in the end, and so her life didn't count for anything."

He patted my bare shoulder. "If you look at it like that, then no life counts for anything. We all come to nothing in the end."

"I guess. I'm tired now."

"Don't fall asleep yet. Let me have one more cigarette."

It was one of Luca's unjustifiable peculiarities that he wanted for us to fall asleep and wake up exactly at the same moment. Together. Needless to say, this rarely, if ever happened and I know it disappointed him.

"Someday you're liable to set the house on fire. Every bit of it's wood. It'd go up easy enough."

"I'll not set it on fire," he assured me. "Tell me what it was like for you growing up. I can't imagine you as a child. I think of you as springing from your mother all grown up."

"I don't really remember being one," I told him honestly.

"Nothing at all?"

"A bit here, a piece there."

"What do you remember?" He was interested now.

"Being afraid."

"What of? The things that children fear? Ghosts? Monsters?"

"I never feared the dead. I can tell you that," I answered, thinking back to the night I had dragged Jesse's body and buried it. No nightmare of him rising from his shallow grave had ever tormented me.

"Then what?" Luca persisted.

"The living. I fear the living."

"But who exactly? Tell me."

"Oh, go to sleep. You ask too many questions."

"I ask because you'd never tell otherwise. Tell me the first time you can remember ever being afraid," he said, trying a different tack.

"That's not so hard," I said. "There was only the one time really, and I never forgot it. There was this man once, who wore a uniform. I think he was a soldier, but I can't be sure."

"What did he look like?"

"I don't remember. I only know he was big. Or else I must have been very small then, because in my memory, the man is very big, like a giant. It was night. Like this night. Hot. So hot that the sheets stuck to me. Just like now. I was sweating."

"Go on," he encouraged me. "It was night and you were just a little girl. Then what happened?"

"Sounds. Like crying coming from my mother's room. I got up and went to the door and listened. She was crying and so I went in and there was this man. They didn't notice me right away but when they did, the man stood up real quick and put on his uniform. My mother stayed on the bed huddled against the headboard. Her face was turned away from me. The man came toward me. He looked mad. I wanted to run back to my room, but I didn't want to leave my mother. I wanted us both to get to my room and lock ourselves in. I knew about locks. I couldn't quite reach the one on my bedroom door, but I knew how it worked. You slid the bolt across. The man was standing over me. I ran past him to the bed. Only when I got into bed with the woman and she turned around, it wasn't Jewel at all. It was this horrible creature with paint all over her face. Her hair was like Jewel's a little but that was all. Everything else about her was different. She had a mouth like a fish, and it was rouged red. She started to laugh, and I ran and ran until I was back in my room. The man was coming after me. I could hear him. I tried to reach the bolt, but I wasn't tall enough. So I dragged over a chair, all the while hearing him coming closer and closer. Just as I got it across, he rattled the knob, and I heard the woman with the horrible face laughing again. 'Leave her alone,' she said to him. 'Her mother says she's afraid of strangers.'"

Luca put his hand on my forehead. "You're so warm," he said. "Are you feverish?"

"No. It's just the heat."

"Did you ever find out who those people were?"

"No."

"Did you ask Jewel?"

"No."

"They must have been guests at the inn," he reasoned. "And Jewel must have let them have her room for the night. But they don't sound like the kind of people anyone would want staying in their home."

"This was never a home to Jewel," I said, unable to keep a certain note of bitterness out of my voice. "It was a place where all wayfarers were welcomed, and we were just here to clean and cook for those wayfarers, no questions asked. I guess that's why I always slept with one eye open."

I felt Luca's hand brush my cheek. "You don't feel that way now, do you?" he said.

"No," I lied.

"Because I never want you to be frightened of anything again. Whatever happens I will always protect you."

Turning, I smiled at him, but it wasn't a real smile. "It's not always that simple, this protecting people. I learned that living with Jewel. I used to beg her to keep her door locked. She never listened, even went so far as to have the lock taken off completely. I guess that was to prove to the guests how much she trusted them, which was ridiculous since she didn't really know any of the people who tramped through here. But I thought that maybe one day somebody wasn't going to live up to her faith in them and maybe they'd take a notion to cut her throat. And there wouldn't be a damn thing I could do about it. So I started taking Caroline into my room at night and locking the door behind us. I got a little crazy about it, kept checking the lock again and again. But we were safe at least.

"Then Jolene was born, and there was somebody else to worry about, to take care of, to protect. When Jolene was an infant, Jewel kept her in a cradle beside her bed so that she could feed her during the night. Jewel would let any old vagrant that wandered by play with the baby and kiss her. I didn't like it. Jolene was her baby, but she was my sister, too, and I had a responsibility to her. But there was so little I could do. Jolene had to be with Jewel so she could feed her. So I started staying awake nights and listening, just in case something should happen, in case somebody might try to hurt the baby or take her away. It was hard to stay always vigilant, always alert, and sometimes I'd nod off… It got to be that I wished Jolene had never been born."

"Darcy, you're shaking," Luca said, putting an arm around me. "You don't have to be afraid anymore." His voice was soothing. "I'm here now. I won't let anything bad happen, I promise."

And I relaxed in the gentle warmth of his folded arm, and I wished he could keep his promise, and at the same time, knew it wasn't his to keep because no one can promise you safety in a world that by its very nature is dangerous.

Time passed, and it was beautiful in the passing. In summer, we went up to the quarry to swim. There was never anybody there but us. People in Galen were too superstitious to swim in a place where a child had disappeared, no matter that it had happened years and years ago. They were still afraid of the watery world that was believed to exist in the depths of the black quarry where Jewel had taught us undines, the water spirits, lived. Sometimes in the evenings, we would go to where Jewel was buried and put flowers by her headstone. Luca had fenced it in very nicely and we weeded it regularly. Now Jewel's was the only grave but someday, I thought, Luca and I would be there with her. From my *Rubaiyat*, that I had memorized by heart long ago, these words came to mind: *And we, that now make merry in the room they left, and summer dresses in new bloom, ourselves must we beneath the couch of earth descend ourselves to make a couch—for whom?* Then we turned back for home and to cheer myself, I made myself think: *Ah, make the most of what we yet may spend, before we too into the dust descend.*

In the fall, we picked apples from the orchard and made cider. We brought in the pumpkins we'd planted too. Neither of us liked squash all that much but pumpkins looked so cheerful both in the field and on the porch that we couldn't resist having a pumpkin patch. One day, Luca picked the bittersweet that grew all around the inn and he filled my arms with it. Every day at dusk, we walked down the lanes, kicking up leaves and watching geese form a black arrow against the sky. After harvest, the fields were barren and haunted, like people newly poor, with the memory of plenty lingering still. At the end of the day, we'd sit on our porch piled with pumpkins and bittersweet, in our rocking chairs, and I'd think that I couldn't wait for us to be old together, old with all the travails of youth behind us. Then, we'd rock and rock and hold hands and fall asleep in our chairs, our hands still joined.

When winter came, we tried to seal up the cracks in the old windows, but the draft managed to get through and the house was always cold no matter how many fires were going. To keep warm, we'd get under blankets and tell ghost stories. I told him about the undines that lived in the quarry, and he told me about werewolves that prowled the Apennines. Once, we were so successful in spooking each other that when I heard a noise downstairs, I made him go down to see what it was. Probably it had been no more than a family of mice looking for shelter from the cold night. But Luca took it all very seriously and in a grave manner, he went to the closet and came back wearing a saber, tied with a sash around his waist. Walking toward the bed, it banged awkwardly against his legs. "It belonged to my grandfather," he told me solemnly, and bravely he went downstairs to confront the intruders.

But there was nothing there to run through with a sword and he came back up a little disappointed. That was when the sight of him stark naked, with this relic hanging from his hip sent me into uncontrolled laughter, and I kept laughing in spite of his begging me to stop, until finally he crawled into bed without a word and, covering me with himself, made me stop laughing for the rest of the night.

In April, I knew for sure I was going to have a baby. Luca acted very silly about the whole thing, kissing and patting me every time I walked by him, even if it was fifty times a day, and smiling at me all the time and looking swelled up with pride, as if he'd done something that every other healthy man in the world couldn't do, and tweaking my nose and pinching my cheek, and in general, making a terrible nuisance of himself. As for me, I still wasn't over the shock of being pregnant. Not that I was dumb to the ways of nature. I knew that if you did certain things long enough and with as much enthusiasm as Luca and I did them, that sooner or later, you were bound to have a baby. It was just that I had never thought of myself as anyone's mother before. Hell, I had only begun thinking of myself as female a scant few years before. But just the same, I loved being pregnant.

During that time, I was reminded of a dress that Jewel had had when I was just a little girl. It was made of velvet and it was her favorite dress that she wore only on special occasions, usually when the railroad men were visiting. I loved that dress. It stirred my senses so. I loved to look at Jewel in that dress because she looked so beautiful, not like someone's mother but like a fairy princess. But the thing I loved most about the dress was the feel of it. I would sit beside her by the hour and just glide my hand along her arm to feel that soft, deep velvet, until she would say in exasperation, "Stop it, Darcy. You're gonna make a bald spot."

My days carrying the baby were like that dress, deep, soft velvet days, when I felt peaceful and peaceable. Time passed serenely, and I learned not to be frustrated at the growing clumsiness of my body, but instead to let myself slow down to that dreamlike pace.

We were lazy in those days, Luca and I. Me, because of the baby. And him, because of me. I'd lie in the hammock and he would sit by my feet and fan me when it got very hot in late August. And he'd watch me. So intently. Like the changes in my body were a show staged just for him. He thought the whole business was very mystical, and he seemed determined to let no aspect of the process pass him by. Having grown large and silent with contentment, I felt like the Sphinx, and that was how Luca seemed to see me too. Full of awe, he'd look at me like I was a natural wonder and say things like, "You have life in you. You are holding the secret to life right inside you."

In my last months, his reverence got on my nerves so that one day I snapped, "I'm not the Virgin Mary and it's no different than cats and dogs! Now leave me alone."

But it was different than cats and dogs, and I didn't ever want him to leave me alone.

Luca was so anxious to meet his child that when he heard the first cry, he rushed in and scooped the baby up in his arms before the midwife had a chance to clean her up. She was beautiful to him even all bloody like that.

I'd figured all along it would be a girl and I thought for sure that Luca would be very disappointed. But he wouldn't have had it any other way. He was so glad of his daughter that I thought he would burst. The way he doted on her, he did everything but nurse her, and I think he secretly cursed nature that he couldn't do that. He loved to watch me nurse and I loved to have him watch me.

When I asked Luca what he wanted to name her, he said he would let me decide, and with unusual largesse, I said I wanted to name her Renata, after his mother, which was quite a sacrifice, since I thought it was an ugly name and not even American. He was so touched at that, he almost cried, and I was glad I offered. Secretly, I made up my mind that she'd be Renata on paper only. I'd call her Rennie, and no one need ever know the origin of the nickname.

There's nothing quite so vain or quite so much fun as searching your child for parts of yourself. At six months old, we could see that Rennie was her father's daughter. It was all there, the dimples, the long dark lashes over warm blue eyes, the thick, dark hair. I was glad of it too, and not just because Luca was prettier than me. Really, it was because he had been orphaned young and besides me and Rennie, he didn't have anybody. So it was good that he could find proof of himself, that he indeed did exist, in his child. But though she was her father all over again in appearance, she took little else from either of us. It was Jewel who had made her mark on the granddaughter she would never know. The resemblance was not in the face or in the eyes, but rather in what lay behind the eyes. That same sweet wistful way in which she looked out at the world but was never changed by it. She was just a baby yet, but I got the feeling that nothing that came to her in life, no matter how sordid, would ever mar that deep, abiding innocence. And there was something else harder to describe, a sort of fey quality that made me think she knew fairies and possibly they talked to her.

Before the baby, I'd been afraid that things would change between me and Luca, that maybe he would be like some men and not want me until it was time for the next baby. That would have been like death to me. But I was wrong. Our nights were different only in that somehow, they were more intimate. There was a kind of communion now that had not been there before, for all our closeness. Now there was truly a cord that bound us, a tangible one that would continue to exist long after we were gone. And I loved him so, though I never said it, loved him with a conviction that I would never have thought possible. Luca never told me he loved me either, but I never felt the lack. How could I, when his every touch, his every glance told me so in a way more telling than words? He loved me and more than that, I felt loved, and in my ignorance, I hoped that that would protect us. But I know now that there was something dark moving toward us even then, something older than Luca's love, and something that was far more familiar to me. How did I know this? Because the light always attracts the dark. That's the way of it.

There was no herald. I simply walked into McAllister's Dry Goods Store one morning and there was Aaron stocking shelves. He grinned at me and said, "Hey, Darcy. Long time, no see."

My eyes did not widen in surprise. My face was too disciplined for that, trained from years of forced impassivity. I just walked past him stiffly to the cash register.

Later, I would marvel that Luca had not been with us that day. He almost always was. Sometimes we went to McAllister's because we needed something. More often, just for the walk. But always together, except for today. Luca's bad leg was aching, and he hadn't felt like walking.

"Did you come to buy something, Darcy, or just to stare at my hardware?" It was Mr. McAllister. He'd always been gruff with me but never mean.

"Sorry," I said. "I was just kind of surprised to see Aaron here. He's been away so long."

He looked over my shoulder to make sure nobody was about. We could hear Aaron across the store stacking lumber. "He's back all right. Got himself dishonorably discharged from the service. Some trouble over a girl. Broke her arm or something."

"Why'd you hire him?"

The old man looked at me like I was the stupidest person on earth. "Isn't that plain as a turd in a punch bowl? He came in wanting a job and I don't want to lose my store. Know what I mean?"

"Sure, but—"

"Come on now, girl. You've lived here all your life. You can't be thinking it's coincidence that every time somebody has words with Aaron, his house catches fire."

"You mean—"

"It ain't lightning. Quiet—"

Aaron walked up to the counter brushing sawdust off his clothes. "And who's this pretty little thing," he asked, bending down to Rennie.

Rennie gave him a big smile and reached her arms up to be lifted. Nearly three years old now, she was a friendly child who liked to be held by everybody, without discrimination, from Mr. McAllister to the postman.

Aaron extended his arms too, but before he could touch her, I jerked her little arm and snapped her back to my side. She started to cry. I'd never been rough like that with her before.

"Don't cry," Aaron said, taking her by the shoulders and turning her around to face him. "Come on and smile for your uncle Aaron."

I felt a wretching sensation and thought I might vomit, but I kept still. I was afraid of him now. Now, I had so much, so very much to lose. "We've got to go," I finally managed to say, and walked past him and out of the store.

"So long there, Darcy," he called after me. "Be seeing you around…I promise."

Luca knew as soon as I came home that something was wrong. I told him about Aaron being back from the service. He knew I hated Aaron, but he never knew why. Luca thought I hated him because of the old feud between the reverend and Jewel. I would never tell him the truth. Luca was cursed with a heroic temperament, something I saw as a character flaw that experience had taught me often led to disaster. For his part, he had never forgotten the fight he'd had with Aaron at the Harvest Moon Dance a hundred years before in school.

"I'm never going to McAllister's again," I said, thinking to appease him. But it just made it worse.

"You certainly will go there!" He turned on me. "And so will I. We've been going there for years and I'll be damned if I'm going to change my life to avoid Aaron Hamilton."

Luca was as good as his word. The very next day, he insisted we all go to the store as we always had. I hoped fervently that Aaron wouldn't start talking to Rennie again, or God forbid, touch her. I knew Luca would kill him then, or try to, and in the trying, be killed or hurt himself.

I caught sight of Aaron as soon as we entered. He was marking tools and when he saw us, he came up brazenly, but something in Luca's manner must have given him pause because he stopped abruptly before he got too close. It was strange with Luca. He was more threatening when quiet than others are in a temper. Aaron closed his mouth, and when he opened it again, it was to say only a casual, "Hello, folks. Can I help you?" But even that was more than Luca was willing to take.

He grabbed Aaron by the throat and backed him into a pile of lumber. "I don't want you around my wife," he said. "And I don't want you around my child. Do you understand that?"

Aaron didn't seem to have the good sense to be afraid, despite having his wind cut off like that. "I didn't know she was your wife," he said, but not in apology. Instead, he seemed only amused that we had married.

"Well, now you do. So stay away from me. Stay away from my family and my house. If I catch you anywhere near the inn, I'll kill you," Luca told him, without further elaboration. With that, he let go of Aaron and hurried both of us out of the store.

He wouldn't speak to me all the way home, and when we got back to the inn and I tried to take his hand, he flung me off. "Rennie's taking a nap," I said. "We could go upstairs and—"

"Not now," he said, crossing the room in long angry strides, his hands thrust into his pockets. "How can you think of that when we've been insulted this way?"

"Aaron didn't insult us, Luca. He hardly spoke to us."

"It was his manner. He didn't have to speak. He was taking your clothes off with his eyes."

Another girl, a younger girl, a girl who didn't know things, would have been flattered by her husband's jealousy. I was just afraid. "Can't we just forget this day?" I pleaded with him.

"Forget it?" He turned to me with renewed fury. "You think I'm afraid of him, don't you? You think I'm afraid of Aaron Hamilton."

In that moment, I saw how very young Luca was and how very little he knew about what mattered and what didn't. "I don't think any such thing. But—"

"But what?"

"But I think you should be afraid. I love my life. I never thought I'd live to say that. But I love my life with you and our child. I won't risk that for anything, certainly not to prove that you're not afraid of him. And that's why we have to stop parading through McAllister's just to show we can."

He looked at me with contempt, but I wouldn't stop talking. "Don't you see? Aaron isn't right in the head. He never has been. Maybe the reverend made him that way. Maybe he was born that way. I don't know. I don't care. For whatever reason, the Hamilton boys were always crazy. Everybody knows that. They never cared about their own lives or anybody else's. Aaron'll kill you as soon as say good morning. That's why you just got to stay out of his way until he gets tired of this and hops a train to go torment somebody somewhere else. It's the only way."

"It's not my way." His jaw hardened and through his teeth, he said, "I'm not a coward, Darcy, and now I see that you are."

I went and put my arms around him and my forehead against his shoulder. "Only about you. I couldn't keep on without you. I'd sooner die."

"Stop it!" He shook me off.

"Please, I'm not asking you to hide from him. Just don't seek him out. If you care for me, you'll do that much. I know Aaron. You can only imagine him."

It wasn't in Luca to refuse me much, and I felt him soften. He kissed my forehead and lifted my chin. "All right, Darcy. We won't go there anymore. But know this. If ever I see him near the inn, I'll kill him, even if it means spending the rest of my life in prison. There are some things worse than dying. Do you understand?"

I nodded and kissed both his dimples, but I knew then, as I had always known, that it would be no challenge of Luca's that would draw Aaron to the inn. It would be me.

7

The Rest Is Lies

It was coming, coming, had been coming all along. Just like Jesse, for surely it hadn't started the day he had set foot on the porch steps. Surely it had begun long before that. When? Maybe the day he'd stolen a motorcycle, thinking to hide. Or the day he'd jumped ship. Or the day he left wherever it was he'd come from. Or the day he was born.

It had been coming all along. I know that now. Each clock at the inn, and there were many because Jewel loved clocks, ticking off the seconds one by one until the day arrived. Everything waiting, waiting for the proper month in the proper year on the proper day at the proper hour. It had been coming all along. I knew it. And yet I was still surprised.

Remembered well, too well, for later I would relive it again and again in waking dreams. Everything. My nausea. Strange. There'd been none with Rennie. But this second child had given me a sick feeling since conception. Maybe he was already protesting being made to enter the world. The weather, hot and heavy, and unnervingly still, threatening thunder. What I wore. What Luca wore. Everything I did that evening..

We'd had a scrawny chicken for dinner, and after the dishes were put away, I had gone up to put Rennie to bed. I waited while she said her prayers. I'd always thought the benefit of prayer dubious, but Luca, who was comforted by ritual, insisted she recite a prayer each night the nuns had taught him: "Angel of God, my guardian dear, to whom God's love commits me here…" Whenever Luca and I were getting along too well, we could always get into a rousing argument over religion. Our

Gods were very different deities, and always his was kinder than mine.

After prayers, I kissed her goodnight and went downstairs to Luca. He was waiting for me on the front porch, smoking a pipe. I think he thought it made him look older and more sophisticated. I liked the smell of pipe tobacco, and every now and then, he'd pass it to me so as I could take a puff.

"I wish we could put a lock on Rennie's door," I said. It was an old request, but every once in a while, I'd bring it up again.

"I thought we'd been through that before," he said wearily.

"We have. But what if a stranger should get into the house? He could just walk right into her room and take her while we slept."

"Darcy, you can't live your whole life expecting thieves and kidnappers. We have nothing anyone wants. Caroline took away everything that was worth anything and kidnappings only happen to rich children. Besides, if we locked her in, how could she get out to tell us if she was sick or had a nightmare or something?"

"Then why can't she sleep in our room?" I persisted.

I watched him refill his pipe. "We've been over that too. The child likes her privacy. She doesn't want to sleep with us. She'd rather—"

And then it happened, like a clap of thunder or the strike of a copperhead. A hand coming out of the bushes, a hand with a piece of pipe or a crowbar. Too dark to see. A lunge forward. Luca too startled to fend off his attacker, slumping forward, his pipe clattering to the porch floor. Aaron uncoiling himself. Me, starting to rise, pressed back into the chair. Then suddenly everything still again, set in our new positions, like musical chairs.

Aaron stood before me, his hands on his hips, smiling. "Nice night," he said. "Lots of lightning bugs."

I had to think. Think. But I was too confused. My brain scrambled to grasp what had happened, what was happening—but not what was going to happen. That was too awful to consider, and I resisted the foreknowledge even as I sensed what he'd come for.

"I've missed you, Darcy," he said, resting his weight on one leg, with the other against the seat of my chair. With his foot, he rocked it. "You don't come around the store no more. I've thought a lot about you these past years. Remember when we were kids?" He stopped to pick up Luca's pipe, and finding it still smoldered, he relit it. "Remember how we used to play together. They were the best times. I knew you were mine, that you'd always belong to me. We're alike, you and me." He smiled. "Hell, no one else ever wanted you. You were my secret and I knew no matter how long I was gone, I could count on you waiting for me." The smile left his face. "You oughtn't to have married him. He's a stranger here, and not like us. We're different. We're tough and we know it. We make people bend to us, even if we have to bully them to do it. You ought not have married," he repeated. "Why'd you do it?"

The power to speak had not returned yet, and I could only stare at him in silent terror.

"Why?" His face twisted in rage and he reached out to prod me with the length of metal.

"I—I love him."

Sudden laughter. "Well, I think you're a widow now." He motioned in Luca's direction and before he could stop me, I went to the still form. Quickly, Aaron wrenched me to my feet but not before I felt the subtle rise of Luca's chest. He was still breathing.

"Get upstairs." Aaron poked me with the pipe.

"What do you want with me?" I asked, but of course I knew.

The grin spread across his face. "What I've wanted since we were ten years old," he said. "Now get up those steps or I'll go alone…to see that little girl of yours."

The mention of Rennie propelled me forward. "Leave her. She's a baby."

Again, soft laughter behind me. "Not such a baby. You weren't all that much older when you started running this place."

We had reached her door now. "Please," I said in a last effort.

"Open it."

I could hear her breathing as he pushed me towards the bed. Looking down at her sleeping, my own breath caught. Aaron looked down at her, too, and there was a tenderness in his expression that was at odds with all I knew him to be. "Beautiful child," he said. "Looks just like the Eye-talian. If I'd had a face like that, there's no telling what I could have been in this life."

He bent and touched her dark hair. She stirred and called, "Mama," rubbing her eyes sleepily.

"It's all right," he said soothingly. "I just come for your mama and I'll be on my way. You go back to sleep."

He pulled the coverlet up to her neck and then his eyes came up to meet mine. "Where's your bedroom?" I didn't answer. "You're shaking." He seemed surprised. "Are you afraid of me, Darcy?"

"Yes."

"You never were before."

I flinched as he raised his hand to brush a strand of hair from my face. "I didn't have Luca and my girl then."

He nodded sympathetically. "Takes all your courage away to have something to lose. Just the opposite with me." He began pushing me out of Rennie's room and down the hall. "I guess I'm 'bout as courageous as a man can be. This it?"

I didn't answer but some sick intuition must have told him so because he pushed me through the door, to stand square in front of me, feet apart, eyes squinting appraisingly. "You grew up to be a fine-looking woman," he said, "which is amazing seeing as how plain you were."

Without forethought, I said, "It's because I'm loved." It was something Luca had told me long ago, that to him I would always be beautiful, even someday when all that others might see was a very old woman. I'd almost forgotten.

"What?" He looked at me sharply.

"Nothing."

"Don't cry," he ordered. "I won't hurt you unless you make me."

Until that moment, I hadn't even realized I was crying.

He went and lit the lamp. It made shadows dance on the walls. He put his hands on my shoulders and smiled close to my face. "You're like a Christmas package waiting to be unwrapped…"

Christmas. I thought of last Christmas. Luca had given me a pearl drop necklace that had belonged to his mother. Then he'd gotten mad at me for telling Rennie there wasn't any Santa Claus. Finally, we'd agreed that there really wasn't any magic left in the world, though we could never agree just when the magic had gone out of it. Christmas.

His hands were on me now, and I gasped as he ripped the front of my dress open. I heard the buttons rolling across the floor as he pushed me onto the bed and got on top of me.

I lay perfectly still as he moved against me. Somehow, I must get through this. Just please God, don't let Luca wake up. Not yet. Then suddenly there was another sound that drowned out Aaron's groaning. It came muffled at first, strange, not human. Then closer, deep and throaty, not so unfamiliar now. Still, I couldn't place it. Aaron shifted his weight off me so he could see where the sounds came from. My eyes followed his and what I saw amazed me. Sam hovered by the doorway. He was a hundred years old now, but it seemed he had not forgotten the chivalry of his youth. The fur on his back stood straight as porcupine needles, and his ears lay flat against his head. What teeth he had left were bared, and showed dirty yellow beneath his gums. With amazing speed for an animal his age, he crossed the room and the shout that escaped Aaron told me that he was being bitten.

I did not need to think now, for in fact thought was useless. Instinct drove me down the hall. Instinct told me what I must do. The shotgun was still where we had left it since our last hunting trip, hidden in one of the guest room closets. The bullets weren't there and vaguely I remembered I had hidden them separately. I was conscious of the sound of Aaron being mauled in the other room, of the dog's growling frenzy, of Aaron cursing, and finally of a sharp whimper that preceded the silence.

Where were the bullets? Clothes, hats, shoes rained down on me as I tore the closet apart. Damn Luca. He wouldn't let me keep it loaded because of Rennie, and now…

I remembered suddenly. The drawers to Jewel's old dresser were so heavy that they were hard to open. Eight drawers. They were not in the first. Aaron coming down the hall now. He had a heavy step for a man his size. I could hear him opening and closing doors. The bullets were not in the second drawer. Maybe Luca had moved them to another room entirely. *Please, God, please.* The dubious benefits of prayer. *But please, God, anyhow.*

"Darcy." A singsong voice. "Wh-e-r-e a-r-e y-o-u?" A hide and seek voice, the voice of childhood.

Son of a bitch. My hand closed over the heavy metal box. Here it was. With trembling fingers, I loaded the gun. The moon gave the only light in the room, but nothing in me hesitated. Loading this gun in the dark, shaking with a fear as old as I was, was something I had done a hundred times before in my mind, anticipating.

When it was loaded, I got up and turned on the electric light so there would be no chance of missing him. All at once, he was illuminated in the doorway, the light momentarily blinding him. I backed up until I felt the support of the wall against my back.

"I've got a gun, Aaron. I'm going to kill you."

He looked at me surprised. "Kill me?" he said, his voice filled with disbelief. "But we're childhood sweethearts. Friends forever."

"No," I said, surprised at my own calm. "We were never friends. I had no father, no brothers, and you thought you could do whatever you wanted to me." The disbelief in his eyes was giving way to fear. He was afraid, and his fear stirred something deep within me that made my fingers tingle with pleasure. "But

I don't need a father or brothers." Stroking the barrel of the gun, I watched him back away. "I have this." Confused, his eyes cast about for a way to leave, and in a gesture of abject surrender, he raised his palms to me, exposing them, and turned to walk away.

Time did strange things then. It stopped and it seemed like I had all the time in the world to make up my mind. If I was an animal and I wasn't planning to eat him, I'd have let him go. Surrender would have been enough for an animal. It wasn't enough for me. An animal cannot think about the future. He cannot fear it. If he is safe for the moment, it is enough. It wasn't enough for me. I didn't want Aaron Hamilton hurt. I didn't want him imprisoned. I wanted him dead, so dead that he could never again touch my child's hair, or make my husband feel less than a man. If he were to live, I would never stop being afraid. I would not show it, would deny it, but I would be afraid. And I could not stand myself afraid. No.

I had so many reasons, real justifiable reasons to kill him, reasons that you would accept and say to yourself that I was within my rights to kill him. Jewel used to say that every dog was God and that was why 'dog' was 'God' spelled backwards. It was just one more of the idiotic theories she had developed growing up among hillbillies, first in Texas and then in Galen. Still.

In the end, I didn't kill him for any of the reasons that might make it right and square me with heaven. I didn't do it for my husband or my child or because Aaron had raped me. I killed him because he killed my dog and the fact is you cannot kill a person's dog and expect that person to let you live.

I walked, unhurried and sure, out of Jewel's room and down the hall and stood and braced myself against the rail of the second-floor landing.

Aaron was going, had just reached the door and was passing through, when I took deliberate aim, bracing myself for recoil. I raised the barrel and fired. I shot him in the back, for no other reason than that was the side facing me in the moment. He fell forward onto his face and I knew that he wouldn't get up again.

And yet it wasn't enough. So I cracked open the shot gun and slid the second bullet I held in my palm into the chamber and shot his dead body again. Only it still wasn't enough. So I took the last bullet I held and loaded it and shot his dead body a third time. That was enough. It had to be. I had no more bullets. Then I laid the gun beside me and sat down on the step. Aaron was dead and the fear was gone, and with it all emotion.

From the corner of my eye, I saw a ball of brown fur, and summoning what strength I had left, I got up and went to kneel beside Old Sam. Blood had matted on his head where Aaron had crushed his skull. My poor boy. He had not the human concern for himself to know better than to give his life for mine. Poor simpleminded creature had gone after Aaron with no other thought in his dog's brain but to save his mistress who had never wanted him in the first place. And sitting with his bloody head in my lap, I did what I had not been able to do for Jewel. I cried. I had a right to mourn him. After all, it was me had taken care of him long after the novelty of a dog in the house had worn off for everybody else. I wondered if he'd known how I felt about him, even though I'd taken his presence for granted and hadn't paid any more attention to him than I had a piece of the furniture.

There was the creak of stairs being climbed and then a heavy hand on my shoulder. Luca was standing there.

"He killed him," I said dully.

Luca looked at me uneasily, as if he didn't know me.

"Why'd he do it? The dog bit him, yes, but he was so old. Hardly had any teeth to speak of. So why'd he—?"

"Stop it, Darcy." Luca knelt beside me. "Let the dog down. You've got blood all over your dress."

"Blood," I repeated, trying to attach the word to the substance. Then a memory and I said, "Do you remember the first day you came here? I had blood on me then, too, chicken's blood. Or was it pig's? We ate it for dinner. Do you remember?" It seemed very important to me that he remember.

He was about to speak when Rennie's door opened, and she

came flying out of her room and into his arms. She must have heard the gunshots because she was crying and talking incoherently. Luca carried her back to bed and when he came back, I had not moved. So he lifted the dog off me and made me stand.

"Aaron's dead." He stated the obvious.

"I know. I shot him. Thrice." Already it seemed like something that had happened a long time ago.

"Did he…hurt you?"

I knew what he was asking, and I clutched the front of my dress together and I said, "No." And then to be more convincing, I added, "He didn't have time." I lied to him. Yes, and not just a lie of omission like with Jesse. I lied to him. But I lied *for* him, too. He could not have stood the truth. He would hate me for it. He would hate himself for hating me, but he was still such a boy that he would not be able to keep himself from hating me, from hating us. The truth would be unlivable. Then, like all liars, I changed the subject to something innocuous and moot: "But I had a terrible time finding the bullets. Promise me we'll keep it loaded from now on. Promise me."

"Darcy," he said gently. "Tell me how it happened. You shot him in the back."

"I had to. He'd have come back. He always came back."

"I'm going for the sheriff."

"No. We can hide him. We can bury him. It can be done. I know. They rot very quickly in the heat."

He looked at me incredulously. "You don't know what you're saying." His voice was losing patience. "Don't worry," he said more gently. "He attacked us. We'll find justice."

"There is no justice." I looked at him hard. "There's just us."

"Don't talk like that. It would be murder."

"It's already murder, Luca."

"It's not. You killed him to protect yourself and Rennie… and me. Didn't you?"

I felt very tired now and everything he said seemed to come from a great distance and to take a long time to reach my ears, like something heard under water. Even the prospect of prison didn't seem so bad so long as they let me sleep. I still had fond memories of reform school. Maybe prison would be like that. Maybe there'd be a prison library with encyclopedias. "All right," I said at last. "We'll tell the sheriff everything. I'll tell him I shot Aaron and—"

"No," he said, and I looked up to stare at his determined face. "You will say nothing. I will do all the talking. They'll never know it was you who shot him. No one will ever know that. Everyone will think I did it— Don't interrupt me. For once, listen and do as I say. I couldn't help you when it really mattered, but I can protect you now. That, at least, I can do."

"But I'm not asking you to," I said. "I killed him, and I'll pay for it. I won't let you go to prison—or worse—for something I did."

"It isn't something you did," he said quietly. "It's something I failed to do. And if you think I'd let my son be born in prison, you don't know me at all."

"It might not be a son."

He tried to smile, but it died quickly on his face. "I won't have my daughter born there either."

Then he went out into the night, never to be the same man again.

Maybe if we'd had the money to get Luca a good lawyer, things would have happened differently. After he was arrested, I called up Caroline and asked if her husband could come down and help Luca. But old pocket-watch three-piece-suit told me he was a corporate lawyer and not a criminal lawyer, and when I asked him were there no criminals in corporations, he assured me there were not.

So the court appointed a lawyer for Luca. He was a nice boy, fresh faced and new to his profession. I think he really wanted to help us, but he didn't have much experience and Luca wasn't very cooperative. Knowing himself a poor liar, Luca was afraid to reveal too much and implicate me by accident. The lawyer was afraid to have a trial by a jury of Luca's peers. Luca had no peers really because he was a foreigner, and foreigners made unsympathetic defendants in a part of the country where most of the people looked on anyone who wasn't born and raised there as already suspect. So we gave up the right to jury trial, and everything was left up to the judge.

Until the very end, we kept hoping that Luca would be given a suspended sentence, and maybe he would have been, if not for the one question the judge kept coming back to time and time again: *Why, if Luca had acted only to protect his family, had Aaron Hamilton been shot in the back trying to leave the house, and not once, but three times?*

I could have told the judge some things. That Aaron had tried to rape me once before. That he had watched and waited and stalked me ever since. But why, Luca would want to know, hadn't I told him any of this? In the moment I had told the big lie, I only saw that one lie. But it's never just one lie and soon after, the whole spiderweb of lies I would have to tell presented itself. And even if I'd been willing to tell the truth belatedly, how could I explain why I'd done it? How could I explain that I had never wanted Luca to know those kinds of things really happened in the world, that I had wanted to keep him as one precious and apart from all the ugliness in Galen that only the initiated could see?

In the end, Luca was sentenced to ten years in prison, eligible for parole in five. But I knew as I listened to the judge read his sentence that a part of him, the part I had always loved best, would be imprisoned forever and would never come back to me even when the rest of him did.

They led us to a small outer room so that we could say goodbye before he was taken away. A guard stood by the door, trying very hard not to watch us but curious in spite of himself.

"I'm glad my father isn't alive to see me now," Luca said, the trouble darkening his blue eyes to navy. He looked so old to me, older even than that day he'd returned after the mine accident. "My father had such great plans for me in America. What great things I would accomplish here!" He laughed bitterly and motioned to the guard by the door. "And this is what I've become."

I saw the pain in him and wished I could have taken it from him. I knew what to do with it. You held it at arm's length and never let it touch you. But Luca didn't know that, and he had taken it right into the core of himself where he would brood on it each day in prison, until there would be nothing left but the pain. "You haven't *become* anything," I said. "You're still the man you always were. And five years isn't such a long time."

"It might as well be forever," he said, and I knew there was no comforting him. He was still too young in his heart to take the long view about anything. "Something has changed, Darcy, something we'll never be able to change back."

"Don't say that. Please. It's like a knife in my heart to hear you talk like that. We'll get through this. You'll see. I'll come to visit you as often as I can."

He took my hands and held them against his chest. "One thing," he said fervently. "Promise me you'll never bring Rennie, that you'll never tell her where I am."

"But you can't mean you don't want to see her for five years."

With his head in his hands, his words came out strangled. "Can't you understand? She's my child. Not an hour will go by that I won't think of her." He raised his head pridefully. "But she must never see me in prison, never like that. Promise me."

"All right."

"Thank you." He stiffened and straightened his spine. "Now please go."

We came together awkwardly, both of us feeling the eyes of the guard. Five years would pass before I could hold him again, lie beneath him, feel his body warm from sleep against my own. I wanted to hold him so close that the warmth of him would last that long. Instead, he kissed me lightly on the mouth and pushed me gently and firmly away. I turned around so as not to watch the guard lead him out of the room.

As I left the courthouse, my head bent over and unmindful of where I was going, I ran into a man on the steps. Opening my mouth to excuse myself, the familiarity of the face stopped me. It was a long ago face that the years had changed. Yet something had not changed. The eyes. Wild eyes, with the metallic glint of birds. Eyes like Aaron's. But Aaron was dead. It was Seth Hamilton, Aaron's brother. I froze. It was like finding out Satan had a sibling. He didn't say a word, just stared in a way that went through me, and in his gaze, I saw that he wasn't fooled. Seth knew me. Like Aaron, he had known me all my life. He would know who had really shot his brother. Not once like Luca would have done. But three times. He would know and he would not forget.

The first thing I did when I returned to the inn was to move Rennie's bed into the room Luca and I had shared. After that was done, I screwed two deadlock bolts, one at the top and one at the bottom, into my bedroom door. I could not stop him from coming, but Seth Hamilton would not catch me unawares. I would be as prepared for him as I had been unprepared for his brother. This time, it would be different.

In the next months, Rennie would ask me more times than I could count why her father had gone away, where he was, and when was he coming back, until I thought I would lose my mind. And even when she wasn't asking about him, just her physical presence was a constant reminder that there had been a stranger once, who had loved me, given me a child, and was no longer with us now. When Rennie looked up at me to pose one of her endless queries, it was with her father's face, his eyes, his smile, and she must have wondered why so often I couldn't bring myself to look at her.

If the days were hard without him, the nights were worse. I ached for him in a way that was without sentiment, in a way that had nothing to do with my loftier memories of him, and my pregnancy, now in the fifth month, did nothing to lessen that longing. I remembered too well how he had felt beside me, how when I woke up it was always to feel his arm around me, his leg thrown over mine, as if he could not stand for us to be separated even in sleep. And the things he did to show he loved me, the way he would get out of bed in the middle of the coldest night to get me a drink of water, the way he brought my breakfast to me in bed every Sunday morning, even though I wasn't sick, how comforting he could be after a nightmare, and how funny when I needed cheering, how many stories he had about Italy. Now there seemed nothing left but a drafty old house and a little girl who asked questions for which I had no answers. And always, there was the sense of time passing, time lost, the certainty that things could never again be as they once had been.

Now began the dark hours, when every shadow in every corner of the secretive old house would gather around me like a black cloak of despair. For the first time, I was truly alone, the way I'd always wanted to be. Like all lonely children, Rennie had grown so adept at amusing herself that it was easy for me to forget she was even there.

The days were only tolerable because with Luca gone, there was always something demanding to be done and only me to do it. On Thursdays, I'd go with Rennie to do the marketing. We'd become notorious since Aaron's death, and always there were whispers and stares. Everyone in Galen was satisfied that Jewel Willicker's eldest girl and that dirty little foreign boy had come to no good. Wasn't that just as they'd always predicted? Yet their hate was strangely comforting to me. At least it was familiar, and there was some solace in knowing that some things never changed, that something could be counted on to endure, if only the hate of a small town.

The nights were the hardest. It was just me at night, without even the enmity of the townspeople to pit myself against, to make me forget myself in proving just how indifferent I was to them. The night had a power that the day never had, the power to shatter the picture I'd always had of myself, one as much a fable as anything in a fairy story. Someone so strong, she needed no one, for her strength was not drawn from others, but generated from some place within. Such piffle. Why, it was Jewel who had made me strong. Yes, soft-spoken, affable, and unbendable Jewel. And my sisters. And later Luca. And because they had loved me, they had let me live my whole life through, believing I didn't need them. But I did. I couldn't be strong alone. I needed someone to be strong for. Now there was no one to be strong for but Rennie, and Rennie had her own peculiar kind of strength, that same strange capacity that Jewel had had—to be born new each day.

The day is lost to activity, but the night is still, and in the stillness, truth comes upon you quietly. And in the night, that yawning chasm of time between the early approaching darkness of winter and the first hint of morning light, I discovered the inn was haunted. Not with dead people. Jesse's body was surely dust in the orchard by now. And not by Aaron. Rumor had it his mother had had him cremated. No, the inn was haunted with convictions long held and false, hopes long cherished and crushed, and plans, made with great enthusiasm that would never come to pass.

It had started with Jewel's misconception of innkeeping, the idea that you could take vagrants into your home, feed them if they were hungry, give them a place to sleep when they couldn't pay, and imagine they would not think you a fool, serviceable only to be taken advantage of. Jewel believed that if you were kind, kindness would come back to you, like a pigeon to roost. She had believed this with a conviction that rejected all evidence to the contrary. And she had died believing in all for which she had no logical reason to believe.

And Luca. Come to a new country and imagining the great things his father and he would accomplish there. Thinking, in spite of everything, that it would all turn out well, for no better reason than he wanted it to with all his heart.

And me and Kathmandu.

So the inn was haunted, as are all dwellings where great slaughters have occurred, the slaughter of people and the slaughter of dreams. And here I was, left with the carnage. And worst of all was not the dead dream but the living nightmare. The dreams about Aaron didn't start until Luca was gone, as if Aaron had been waiting in the ether for him to leave before he felt free to come to me. In the dream, Aaron was not dead, not shot, not bloody. He looked hale and hearty and cheerful and when he spoke it was teasingly, like a mean older brother. "Did you keep that dress, Darcy?" he'd always ask. "The one I raped you in?" And I'd say, "No, I burned it, just like I'll burn you if you ever come back." And he'd laugh, and say, "You can't burn me, Darcy. I'm already ashes. But I can burn you." Even that wasn't the worst of it because with the illogical logic of dreams, I knew he was dead and couldn't come back. It was what he threatened to tell Luca that frightened me most. "I'm gonna bend over him at night while he's asleep in prison," he'd say in the dream, "and whisper in his ear that I put my seed in you. That baby's mine, not his, and once he knows that, he'll stop loving you, if he ever really did and you'll disgust him, and your baby will disgust him too… Once I tell him." And I'd wake up in a cold sweat, panting like an animal, and covering my mouth with my hand so as not to wake Rennie in the bed beside me. I knew it was Luca's baby and couldn't be Aaron's. Yet I felt as if the life inside me had been defiled by the rape and that it would, against all laws of biology, somehow also be Aaron's baby I was carrying.

Time was turning in upon itself again. Night after night, I would sit in front of the fire that never warmed me and think, if only Jewel were here. Jewel, needing me to calm her senseless fears, and in calming her fears, my own would ease. Before there'd been Luca, promising that everything would be all right, and disbelieving, I'd been comforted, nonetheless. Only Rennie now. So young. What could she know of haunting? And soon another child born into this haunted world to live in this haunted house, to a mother struggling to keep her wits and a father in prison. Unhaunted child, I thought, asleep in your silent world, so soon to be disturbed for the first time and for always. They should leave you in peace. Nothing should wake you.

There is a kind of delirium to despair, I know that now, and as I went to the sideboard and poured some brandy, an idea came to me, and drunk with despair more than with brandy, the idea seemed the only bit of reason in an unreasonable world. Later, I was to remember it with an agony of regret that no passing of years would ever dull. But at the time, it seemed the wisest and the kindest thing that I would ever do. I drank the brandy down and poured another. We needed it, my unborn child and me because we were so cold. Even our fingers were numb, had lost all feeling hours ago.

If we were never born… The word *if* had never had any place in my vocabulary before, and none in my thoughts. Things were or they were not. Things happened, and you were either destroyed by them or you managed to salvage something. But whatever happened, speculation was a waste of time.

And yet… if we were never born… The question presented itself again, and this time, I answered. *We'd never know about haunting.* It was too late for me. Too late for Luca. Too late even for Rennie. But the baby was still asleep. There was still time. One thing was clear or seemed so then. This child must never feel what its mother was feeling now, never this wretched. I would protect him as I had always done for Rennie. But I remembered that I hadn't been able to protect her, not really, not when it was most important.

She had seen me that night, had seen Aaron. Had heard the gunshot. Had stood, looking through the spokes of the banister, and seen him bloody. Our eyes met so briefly, I'd hoped it was imagination. But I'd never had any imagination. Did she remember that night? Dream about it in between childish concerns? Wonder if her mother was a monster? I couldn't know, and unwillingly, we shared a secret. Just as Jewel and I had done. A secret that would bind my child to me, even as it would separate her from all other children. The sleeping baby must never know what Rennie and I knew.

But what about the other times, a part of me fought against the natural conclusion to this line of thought. *Would you want the child to miss them?* The times of exquisite happiness, like on the first warm day after a long winter, when you feel your heart rise. There were those times too. *But so fleeting, and first you had to endure the winter,* I answered the fading light of myself. *Still there were times*…the light said back, its voice getting dimmer and all the harder to hear, *when you thought it was enough, enough to make it worthwhile.*

And then I answered aloud, "I don't think so anymore."

There was a woman who lived in the woods, not far from the whorehouse, which, looking back, must have been real convenient. Jewel used to mysteriously recite sometimes, "There was an old woman who lived in a shoe. She had so many children she didn't know what to do… So she went to see the woman in the woods." I didn't know the woman, had never laid eyes on her, because like other Galen outcasts, she was only whispered about. I knew only that Jewel hated her "because of how she makes her living," and for the longest time, I couldn't imagine what the woman could possibly be doing in her cottage in the woods to make Jewel, who thought nothing of befriending prostitutes and thieves, hate her so. It was the only time I could remember Jewel seeming to harbor malice, and it gave the woman a deep fascination for me, until in my later years, I found out just what it was she did.

It was after midnight when I made my way into the woods. Snow had fallen earlier, and when I finally found the cottage, I saw that it was covered in white, as were the trees around it, a scene out of a fairy tale.

I knocked and waited, hoping she would not be angry with me for coming so late. Probably she was used to women coming at all hours. Desperation probably never observed any schedule.

When the door was opened cautiously by a white-haired woman, she didn't ask me why I'd come. There was only one reason anyone would.

"Have you brought money?" she wanted to know.

I nodded.

"Let me see it."

I showed her and she told me to get undressed.

"How many months?"

"Almost five."

"Fine. Lay down and we'll start."

"Is five too far gone?" I asked, starting to undress.

She shrugged. "Makes no difference to me. I've done 'em gone longer."

The whole thing didn't take very long, and would have gone even more quickly if I hadn't started crying. It wasn't because she hurt me. I was too numb from the cold and brandy to feel much of anything. But some place in the pit of my brain had resisted the numbness and was already aching.

After it was done, I wanted to rest a minute, but the woman had someone else coming and she told me I would have to leave. And then she said the cruelest thing anyone had ever said to me in my whole life. She said, "It was a boy."

The snow had stopped by the time I left, and the moon shone blue on the clearing. I walked slowly, with great effort. I'd never felt this light before, like the wind might blow me away, and so weary, tired enough to lay down in the snow and go to sleep. I looked down at the new-fallen snow, thinking to find a place to rest, and as I did, I saw the reason for this unrelenting fatigue. I was bleeding to death. I saw it with each step, as a new circle of red formed against the frozen white ground, and opening my coat, I felt my skirt saturated with a warm wetness. I was dying and leaving my daughter alone in a world that I knew from long experience did not care about her, without a father, without anyone, and it was this knowledge that propelled me forward and changed my direction.

I collapsed on the road leading up to the doctor's house, the same doctor who'd sewn Aaron up after I'd cut him with the sickle. In the end, I owed my life to his wife's insomnia and her love of new-fallen snow. She'd been up looking out her window admiring it when she'd spotted me lying in the midst of it as she sipped warm milk in her kitchen.

Morning came unwelcome and found me alive, though I took no pleasure in the fact, and with it came sobriety, not from drink, but from the drunkenness of despair that had a hold of me the night before. I was not despairing now. That had abated, and in its place was left a resignation to existence. I could not live without Luca. That, I had found out soon after they'd taken him from me. But I could exist without him. That much I could do. I owed it to Rennie.

Dr. Lynch came into the bedroom where he'd put me and said, "I should take you to the sheriff and tell him what you did." I hung my head. I half agreed with him. "And I'd do it too...but for your little daughter. Don't worry. She's downstairs in the kitchen. My wife went and fetched her last night."

"I'm grateful."

"I don't want your gratitude. You got to pull yourself together, girl. You got your man in prison and things are hard for you. Well, too bad. Things is hard for everybody nowadays. That's why they're callin' it the Depression and not the Jubilation! You gotta do whatever you have to to get by and pray there's better days ahead. That's all anybody can do—you hear me?"

"I hear."

"And stay away from that Satan's piss you been drinkin'. You'd never have done what you done if you hadn't gotten yourself all liquored up first. Now put these clothes on. They're the wife's. Threw yours out." He got up to leave. "You be grateful for your life, Darcy. Even when it's a curse, it's a gift."

So Rennie and I went home. The son Luca had so long awaited and with so much hope was dead. Gone to join the other faces that would haunt me and follow me for all my days. But you can live being haunted. Most people do. Each day they beat it back, only to have it rise again each night. But they get along. Somehow.

It didn't matter anyway. Nothing mattered. Only Rennie, and one good reason to go on can trump a hundred reasons not to. My daughter, who had her father's face, was alive, and from now on, when those other faces rose up to haunt me, I would beat them back with that.

8

Turns Ashes

The prison where Luca was serving his time was a three-hour train ride from Galen. I had only been on the train a few times in my whole life and every time the motion had made me sick. This time was no different. Halfway through the ride, I had to go to the bathroom to throw up in the toilet. It isn't easy to vomit on target on a moving train, and as it turned out, I threw up on my shoes.

All morning, I had labored over my appearance. I washed my hair and rinsed it with vinegar, because Caroline had told me once that it made your hair shine. Then I wound the ends around rags to make them curl, but defying all my winding, my hair remained straight as a poker. I tried putting it up, but the hairpins kept falling out. So I decided to concentrate instead on what to wear. My own clothes were all old and looked it. But in Jewel's closet, I found the velvet dress that had always been my favorite. Except for being too short at the hem, and too tight in the shoulders, it fit fine. But the memory of how Jewel had looked in it was too sharp, and I put it back in the closet and chose instead a plainer one that conjured no memories.

Having tried so hard to look nice, I got to the prison tired, anxious, and smelling faintly of vomit and vinegar. The stone steps leading up to the prison were cool, and I sat down to steady myself. As I sat there, a man with gray hair who looked like somebody's grandfather came and spoke to me.

"I'll bet you're Mrs. D'Angeli." He smiled and his face crinkled into careworn lines.

I'd never been called that before and I was taken aback, but I nodded.

"Luca talks about you and that little girl of yours all the time. Are you feeling all right? You look a little peaked."

"I threw up on the train."

He laughed but not in a mean way. "I'm the same way on trains. But you'll feel better when you're inside and you see Luca. He's been up since dawn getting ready for you, primping like a girl. He's been looking forward to this since the first day he came in here."

"Who are you?" I finally thought to ask.

"I'm the warden here."

"You don't look like a warden," I said. It was always disturbing to me when people didn't look as they should.

"I suppose not," he said apologetically. "Are you feeling better? Would you like to see your husband now?"

He led me to a long corridor. It was divided by a metal grate, with rows of benches on either side.

Before he left, the warden said, "Take a seat. Luca should be out shortly." Then he called a guard. "Bring Mrs. D'Angeli a glass of soda water." He winked at me. "It'll settle your stomach."

But my stomach wouldn't settle. Unwilling, I kept thinking about Joseph Gibbet. He was one of the people who haunted me. They had an electric chair in this prison. I'd read about it once in the newspaper. What if Luca had been sentenced to death? What if he was behind these walls waiting for his turn? What if Rennie and I never saw him again? Did it hurt to die in the electric chair? How could it not?

I heard him before I saw him, the uneven tread of his one bad leg, and when I looked up, I couldn't stifle the gasp that rose in my throat. He had lost weight, a lot of weight, and they had shaved off all of his beautiful hair. But he had groomed himself as best he could, and it showed in his freshly shaved face and the way he smelled of talc. We smiled at each other cautiously, as if meeting for the first time, and our hands moved to meet through the grate, but they stopped just short of touching.

"How are you, Darcy?" he said with the old propriety that was there even in the midst of intimacy, and I saw him glance at my waist.

"I'm all right. How about you? Is it terrible in here?"

We seated ourselves on the benches. "Not really. No one mistreats me, and the warden has been kind. He told me to act cheerful. He said people don't like sad inmates. They might feel sorry for them but they don't parole them. He says I'm almost certain to be paroled as soon as I am eligible. He knows how much I want to get back to you and Rennie and the baby."

I looked away from him and down at my hands. My palms were sweaty and I wiped them on the skirt of my dress.

"How is Rennie?" he said.

"She's all right." I could see it coming and I wished for a way to put him off. If only I'd been born with Jolene's ability to talk a dog off a meat wagon. She'd have double-talked him until he forgot all about babies. It was probably only the full-cut dress that had saved me so far.

"Does she ask about me much?"

"Always," I answered without letting him capture my eyes.

"And what do you tell her?"

"Not much. That you had to go away for a while." I glanced at him. He wasn't as I remembered. He looked like a defeated old man instead of one in his prime.

In a troubled voice, he said, "That may satisfy her now, but in a year or two, she'll want to know more."

"No, she won't," I said, happy to be able to ease his anxiety, at least in this. "She'll have forgotten by then." And as soon as it was out of my mouth, I knew. The way his face fell, making him look so profoundly old, I knew. "I didn't mean—I only meant that when they're little they forget so quickly."

He shook his head, as if to shake off the hurt. "It's all right."

We were quiet for a while after that, not the nice kind of quiet we had once known together at the inn when we were too content for speech. This was the kind of quiet that makes the mind scramble for words that don't come, and try as we did, we could not fill the silence that divided us as much as the metal grate. If only I could have touched him. If only we could have lain together, everything might have been confessed and forgiven. That was how it had always been with us. Unable to say the things we felt, our bodies had still been eloquent. If only there was no grate between us. All we could have touched was fingertips and that would have made us too pitiful to ourselves, so we each raised a hand only to stop just short of contact.

"You don't look well to me," he said at last. "You should have gained more weight by now. You were much bigger with Rennie."

Avoiding his eyes was no longer possible, and when I slowly raised mine, his were filled with such tenderness and concern that I had to look away again. He didn't suspect, would never suspect what I had done. For Luca, it was a thing too terrible to be even remotely possible.

"I'm not pregnant," I said. There was nothing left to say. His face didn't change immediately. Added to the concern was only a quizzical look, as if what I'd said made no sense. "...I'm sorry. There just isn't any baby anymore."

The truth came to him slowly and he would put off comprehending as long as possible. "You had an accident?"

Why couldn't I lie as I had done the night Aaron came to the porch? That lie had rolled off my tongue easily enough: Aaron hadn't *hurt* me, I'd said. Why couldn't I lie then, at the prison? Why couldn't I say that I had slipped on the stairs? Or had a sudden pain? No. I was a liar but not an indiscriminate liar. I'd lied about Aaron because the truth would have been unlivable. I would tell the truth about the baby because the lie would be unlivable. I shook my head, no.

"Then I don't understand."

Staring down at my lap, I hoped to find something inscribed there for me to say. "There's a woman..." I began. "She lives in the woods around Galen and she...takes care of women who—"

His hand came down on the counter with such force that

the guard stationed by the door turned toward us. "No!" He said the word to silence me, as if keeping it from being told would keep it from being true. His whole body quivered, like a lightning-struck tree before it's brought down forever. "You're lying. You wouldn't do that. You couldn't."

"I did."

He sank to the bench slowly, holding the grate for support, and I wanted more than anything to hold him in my arms—for it was my tragedy, too—and tell him how very sorry I was, how for me, no night was absent dreams of that unborn child. But it was I who had done it, and I knew I was the last person he would take comfort from. I couldn't stand to see him like that—so aware of his powerlessness, his bitter understanding that he could do nothing to affect life beyond the grate.

More wrenching than the angry words was the pleading that followed. "Please, Darcy, tell me. Tell me you didn't." Then he began to cry.

"I can't," I said. It was too late to lie. Though belatedly, I realized that the truth was just as unlivable as the lie would have been. From here, there was nowhere for us to go. I knew that, and with that knowledge came other knowing. Luca would not come back to me. He would go back to Italy to see if he could find something left of warmth, of welcome, of loving familiarity, of goodness and dignity.

Tearing into my thoughts, he sprang up at me with a savagery that was no part of the man I'd known. Clenching his fingers through the grate, he willed me to look at him, and when I did, I saw a feeling so raw it scared me, a hate so personal that I shrank from him, afraid the grate might not hold.

"What if Jewel had done what you did?" he said, his blue eyes shot with blood and tears.

"I wish she had," I said quietly.

"I wish that too." He changed then into someone I did not know, and yet had oddly created, someone not quite human who suffered an animal kind of anguish, undiluted with any thought of salvation. He didn't have to say it. I already knew, had known even before today. But he gave it words anyway. "For the first time, I'm glad to be in prison—" The guard started toward him, alerted by the violence in his voice, in his rage-taut body. "Glad that something keeps me from you. I'd kill you"—he groped in an agony of frustration —"and this whole rotten country!"

The guard motioned to another and together they tried to drag him away, to pry his fingers from the grate, the fingers that once used to entwine themselves in my hair, the fingers that now, without restraint, would have wound themselves around my throat. "Don't come back here ever again!" he screamed as they dragged him away. "Never, never, come back…"

I never did.

9

Back In The Closet Lays

There was nothing mysterious about the way Mr. Sung came into our lives. He came just as all the others had come. On a day in summer, about four years after Luca had gone to prison, with Rennie soon to celebrate—if that word could apply and it didn't—her ninth birthday, he just walked up nice as you please, a little Oriental man in ragged clothes, who barely came up to my shoulder. When he smiled, his slanted eyes completely disappeared. Rennie hid behind my skirt in a fit of shyness.

"You rent room?" he asked.

An old reflex made me snap, "No, I don't rent room. Who sent you here?"

"Men on train," he answered.

Those old goats had never quite gotten it through their heads that Jewel was dead, I thought irritably, and that the inn hadn't taken boarders in years. "Well, those train men are a pack of senile old liars," I told him, pushing a clothespin over the line. "There's no room at the inn." I laughed bitterly at my unintended joke. "So you just go on up the road the way you came and get back on the train. They don't like strangers around here, especially Chinese strangers."

"I not Chinese," he corrected me, smiling. "Korean."

"It's all the same. Whatever you are, I have no rooms to let."

He started to turn away, when some memory of Jewel made me add, "Look, I'm sorry. I'd like to help you. But we're women alone."

He nodded, as if to show me he understood and did not think worse of me for it, and I went back to my laundry. When I turned around again, he was gone.

Rennie stood before me, a little storm cloud. "How could you send him away like that? I don't think he had any place to go."

"Don't be like that," I warned her. "We don't know anything about that Chinaman. He could cut our throats during the night while we slept."

"He could not." She rolled her eyes at me. She was growing up and getting fresh, the way children without fathers often do. "The way you make us sleep together behind a bolted door, Jesus Christ couldn't get to us."

"My, my, what language from a little girl. What would your daddy say if he heard you?"

"He'll never hear me," she said morosely. "He's never coming back. You said so yourself. He's never coming back because you won't write him and ask him to come back."

"It's not that, and you know it." My words were garbled because of the clothespin in my mouth.

"Then why don't you write to him?"

I raised an eyebrow at her. "He doesn't write to me, does he?"

"Well, then, why can't I write to him?" she persisted.

"We've been over this before. I won't have you begging him to come home when he doesn't want to. He wants to go back to Italy. That's where he came from and he wants to go home."

"How do you know what he wants? You haven't seen him in four years."

"You know something, missy, you've had an awful lot to say ever since you turned eight. You were much sweeter when you were seven and if you want to see nine, you better get out of my way before I take a switch to you."

"We don't have a switch."

"I'll make one then."

She rolled her blue eyes to show she wasn't the least bit intimidated. "What about the Korean man?"

"Who?"

"The Chinaman. Can we keep him?"

"He's not a puppy, and more's the pity. A puppy I'd keep," I said, thinking she was Jewel all over again.

"Well, if Papa's never coming back, it'd be nice to have a guest around the inn again. It's very lonely sometimes," she finished wistfully, and the thought of her loneliness softened my resolve.

"Oh, hell, I don't know."

"Please. I just know he will be good for us. Did you see his eyes?"

"Yes. They were slanted and black."

"They were shining."

"I don't know. He's probably back on the train by now."

"He's got short legs," she said. "I can catch up with him. I know I can."

"I don't know. Maybe—but only for a few days." She was off before I could change my mind, her gangly legs a blur of motion. "He better have money to pay," I called after her. "I'm not about to start supporting Chinamen in my old age." But she was already too far to hear.

Later, it struck me odd when Rennie told of how she'd found Mr. Sung again. First, she had gone to the train stop, but he wasn't there. Then she went into the town, thinking he'd be looking for other lodging, but he wasn't there either. Finally, she found him, of all places, sitting on his pack at the bottom of our lane, as if he was waiting for her. And that was how it always was to be with the Chinaman. If you said a thing was red and he knew it was blue, he wouldn't contradict you. Instead he'd just wait in complete faith for the moment he knew would come when you saw it was blue on your own.

I'd never been the curious sort, and other people's peculiarities drew me not at all. But Mr. Sung could have made a stone curious. There was his history, for example—he had none. The little man had come to this country from parts unknown two months before and had taken the train from New York into Pennsylvania, and from there found his way to Galen. He had no family in America, no work papers, and no reason for coming that I could make out. When I asked him pointedly just why he'd come to Galen, he just looked at me with those slanted eyes and said, "I get off boat. I get on train. Men call names. I hear Galen. I say, sound like good place to get off." Beyond that, I couldn't get much out of him. If you asked him something he didn't want to answer, he would turn deliberately dense and claim he didn't understand the question and you could repeat it ten different ways till kingdom come and he would still shake his head like a slow-witted fruit-picker and smile. I considered that he was making a fool out of me by speaking exactly the way I'd always expected a Chinaman to speak, and yet his basic kindness made that a very dim possibility.

Sometimes I thought he was just pulling my leg with the way he talked. His eyes looked considerably more intelligent than his speech and manner would suggest. I would have bet money that if ever I should sneak up on him, I would catch him speaking perfect English, maybe even better than mine. There was something like royalty about him, as if he'd been kidnapped from a palace in China and pushed off the train in Galen. But then, living with Luca had made me touchy about language, so maybe it wasn't so after all.

I learned through Rennie, as I did all the few things I gleaned about Mr. Sung, that his other name was Chun, but neither of us knew which was the first name and which the last. I suppose it didn't matter since it all sounded like pots and pans anyway. For his part, he called me Missus, and nothing I could do would persuade him to call me Darcy.

Even the little man's talents were peculiar. He was always very polite and courteous and glad to do whatever he could around the house. He liked to cook and frequently stank up the kitchen with his concoctions. I wouldn't eat anything that had heads or feet floating around in it, but Rennie, always so finicky before, seemed to like everything that came out of his cauldron.

In spite of myself, I came to appreciate Mr. Sung's slaughtering skills. I'd always made such a bloody, godawful mess of killing chickens and pigs. But the Chinaman knew a much neater way. He simply broke their necks with one quick motion. By killing them first, no blood spurted, only oozed when they were hacked up. I watched, fascinated, as he killed and then expertly butchered them, but I never could master it myself.

Even this unaccountable skill was by far not the oddest thing about the Oriental. Strangest of all were his nocturnal wanderings. Every night, sometime after Rennie and I had gone to bed and lay safe behind our locked door, I would hear the creak of his old mattress as he got out of bed, hear the whine of half-rotted floorboards as he crossed the room, and finally the sound of the front door being softly opened and just as softly shut behind him. Where did he go night after night? Where could a Chinaman go in the middle of the night in Galen? The whorehouse in the woods was the only place I could think of and he seemed too fastidious for that, even if one of the girls had been agreeable.

In spite of all his strangeness, his being a heathen, and that he was only five feet tall, there was a dignity about him that I came to grudgingly respect. A respect, I am certain, that was never returned. Because although he was unfailingly polite to me, I was convinced that underneath it all, he felt only sorry for me and thought his landlady all too fallible. It wasn't that he ever said anything particularly meaningful to me, and certainly never accusing, but still I sensed that somehow, he knew or had guessed just how poorly I had managed my own life and Rennie's. And I resented him for it.

Nor was I happy about the closeness that had quickly sprung up between my daughter and the stranger, and I only let him stay because making him leave would have broken her heart. He'd become her favorite playmate, if not her only soul mate, and often on entering a room filled with their voices, they would suddenly fall silent, as if in a conspiracy of which I had no part.

There was something about him that I didn't like and, moreover, didn't trust. He knew too much, though why I thought this I couldn't say. Our reputation in Galen was practically legend, and I knew better than to think any of the townspeople would stoop to talking with a heathen. But how much had Rennie told him? There was no way of knowing because, in spite of her youth, in this one way, she was her mother's daughter and kept her secrets well.

That September, Galen School had a picnic for the children and their parents. Rennie didn't ask me to go. She knew from experience that I would refuse. I imagined she would go by herself. Strange to tell, the other children and their mothers and fathers never taunted her because of her parentage. But neither did they befriend her. They mostly just kept their distance. I think it was her otherworldliness that gave them pause, as if she might cast a spell and turn them all to frogs. But Rennie didn't choose to go alone. Instead, she went with Mr. Sung. Later, they came back for supper and fell all over each other at the table recounting the day to me. None of the mothers or fathers would talk to the little man, which didn't surprise me. But the children all liked him, except for little Mabel Schuyler, whose mother said that if I was any kind of decent woman, I'd throw the heathen out, and since I continued to let him stay, with no husband in the house yet, it must mean I'd taken to sleeping with Chinamen, in addition to all my other misdeeds. I would have liked to have gone to the picnic and stood in the gazebo on the square and shouted that I indeed had relations with Mr. Sung every day and twice on Saturday nights. But my face never changed, and I didn't say a word when she told me. Secretly, I'd planned to ask him about his board money. He was months behind and had, in fact, never given me another dime after that first day when he'd dropped some money in my hand, looking at the bills as if he'd never seen money before and wasn't sure of its uses. But now, I changed my mind. He probably didn't have any more money and would decide to leave if I pressed him. And those sons of bitches might think I'd thrown him out just to suit them. That would never do. So now he could stay till the second coming as far as I was concerned.

After dinner, I brewed him some of the smelly kind of tea

he liked. "You should go to bed, Rennie," I said. "You're falling asleep in the chair."

"I'm not," she argued, eyes half-closed. "I forgot to tell you. I met a man today."

"What man?" I asked, too quickly, as Mr. Sung watched, sipping his tea.

"His name is Seth. He said he used to know you when you were my age. He was at the picnic, but he didn't have any children with him. He asked if I had brothers or sisters. I said no and he said he didn't have any either. He said his brother had died and his mother had died and now, he didn't have anybody left at all. He was so sad. I felt sorry—"

"Go to bed." I got out of my chair so suddenly that Mr. Sung's tea spilled all over the table, and for a moment I glared at him. He was staring straight at me with the steady gaze and impassive face I'd grown used to. Rennie got up and obeyed me without further argument.

"Were you there today when that man talked to her?" I asked after she had gone.

He nodded. "I don't want him around her." He nodded again. "If you ever see him near her—"

"Don't worry." His face wasn't sympathetic and if he were feeling some emotion, it didn't show on his features.

"I do worry. I'm afraid that—"

"Don't be afraid. He can't reach her."

I didn't understand what "reach her" meant and I assumed it was one of his misuses of figures of speech. I would have pursued it, but he immediately said goodnight and went up to his room.

Days of waiting followed, during which the slightest sound, the slightest stirring, would make me whirl around, ready but never truly prepared, for what was I to do to prepare? Keep the shotgun loaded and by my side at all times? Not sleep? Not let my child play out of my sight for a moment? I decided yes and did all those things as much as possible. I slept like a dog with one eye open and one ear cocked. I didn't let Rennie out of my sight, and it made her hate me a little. I wouldn't even let her go to school. I would rather have her ignorant and alive than educated and dead. And, yes, I carried the shotgun loaded and with me from room to room even though I'm sure Mr. Sung thought I was insane. To his credit, he never called me on it. Instead he acted like it was the most normal behavior in the world.

Then, strangely, things around me began to reflect my fear back at me like a mirror. One night I was reading from *Peter and Wendy* to Rennie as she lay in our bed. "*Was that boy asleep, or did he stand waiting with his dagger in his hand? There was no way of knowing...*"

In those days, I ate, worked in the fields, cared for what little livestock we had, and slept fitfully. But mostly, I waited, for I could smell it in the air, carried on the wind—the sickening smell of revenge long planned and relished. Where would he strike and how? In the house, appearing at a window, or in the orchard, stepping out from behind a tree? With a gun, the way I'd killed his brother, or a knife, hacking away till his rage was spent? And most important, on who would he choose to vent himself? I was the obvious one, but Seth Hamilton, always so much quieter than Aaron, so brooding, would be more devious than that. I had killed someone he loved. Would he take Rennie, thinking to do the same? I could fight him. I would fight him, and if I was killed, it would be with his skin under my fingernails and his flesh in my teeth. But Rennie couldn't fight him. She wasn't waiting. She didn't know enough to be waiting in spite of all my crazy behavior. And in the end, if I was killed, what would happen to her? Would someone in Galen take her in? I doubted it and even if someone did, that would be terrible in itself. She was too strange and fey a child to be raised by anyone but Luca or me.

I decided to write my last will and testament and leave it with Mr. Sung. I read it to him:

I, Darcy Willickers, leave all my earthly possessions to my husband, Luca D'Angeli. It is my final request that my daughter be delivered safely to my husband who currently resides in prison.

I gave the address and directions to Mr. Sung so that hopefully he would take her to Luca. And if they wouldn't let Luca out to take care of his child, maybe that nice warden would take her. But when I tried to communicate all this to Mr. Sung, he got all Chinese about it and refused to understand what I was asking of him. So if I was soon to die, I couldn't even die in peace. It seems like a little thing to ask, to die in peace, but when you really think about it, it's an enormous request and I think few probably are ever able to manage it.

There are so many ways to die, to be killed. Knives to stab, ropes to pull tight, and guns to fire. And so many people to fear and fear for. Who will deliver your end to you? There are the obvious people. The strangers, and knowing their strangeness, we must shun them, lock our doors against them. But what about the others? The familiar ones. The postman, perfectly harmless. Or old man Zook. He'd always liked children. But there was talk once about a little girl… And where and when and how and why? People were so unknowable, even the people you loved. There are so many ways to die. I'd never considered them all before. And if I did methodically consider them all, what then? Then madness. Then, my poor child, forced to trust her safety to a madwoman, one of those to be shunned, doors to be locked against. A madwoman for a mother who could no longer trust herself to recognize the enemy.

In the end, it was time that fooled me. Time passed, a month, then two, then fall turned to winter and into spring, and the spring seemed less dangerous than the winter had been, less dark, less opportunity to hide in the dark. I waited still. But now there were lapses in my waiting, an hour here or there when I let myself sleep or sit down to a meal without thinking of Seth.

And, of course, that was when he came back.

The heart of the night, it was, and sleeping the dreamless sleep of exhaustion, I awakened, disoriented, to thoughts of autumn. Someone was burning leaves in the middle of the night. Coughing, I tried to sit up. Rennie was beside me still asleep. I reached for the gun beside me. It was there ready for me but there was nothing to shoot, and the door was still bolted soundly. I could see it clearly in the flickering glow that softly lit the room. Everything was all right—must be, for the door was still locked. No one had gotten in. We were safe. I coughed again. My breath came labored. The strange light still shone through the window. Not daylight, more like gaslight, but not that either. And the roar of crackling, like a thousand candy wrappers being opened in unison. Then all at once, I knew. The inn was on fire.

Rennie would not wake. I shook her, but the sweet dreamy expression would not leave her face. Trying to get out of bed, I fell to the floor, dizzy, my vision blurring, so that where one door had stood, now there were three and all of them soundly bolted. If I could just get beyond the door to the hallway, get some air into the room. Smoke was everywhere now, thick enough to see, a misty gloaming that brought death. But my legs wouldn't hold my weight, and I had to crawl. Even the floor was warm, and with every inch I gained, I grew weaker. Reaching the door, I touched it. Cool. The flames had not reached the second floor yet. All that lay between us and the life-giving air was the door. The bolts. Two of them. One at the bottom. Every muscle strained to pull it back. Dizziness came in waves, each deeper than the one before. "No one'll ever break this," the hardware clerk had said proudly. The other bolt was near the top. Using the door handle, I pulled myself up and grabbed the knob of the bolt. It would not give. Again, I strained to pull it back and again failed. And the last thing I remember was the defeated sound of my fingernails against the wood of the door as I went down.

10

And Like Wind I Go

When I was once again aware of life, it seemed as if I'd been gone from it for a long time, suspended in some limbo that was like death, but without its finality. But I couldn't have been gone long because the sky was still eerily lit by the burning inn. It was still in flames, its rotting timbers screaming goodbye to those who ran about, trying to bring order to its death throes. Much of the town had turned out to witness the destruction of the dwelling that had so long been the object of their contempt. I think I was the only one who knew that more than the old hotel was burning. A part of our history, my own and that of every soul who had ever wandered or blundered in, was dying too, and with it, the last holdout against ignorant conformity that Galen might ever know. Yet watching it burn, I felt as if a terrible burden had been taken from me.

Sitting up, I heard Rennie crying beside me, a good sound because it was as much the sound of life as laughter. "She's all right," a voice assured me. It was Dr. Lynch, the one who'd found me bleeding in the snow. A good man, that doctor, in snow or flames. "She's just scared. But there's no saving the inn, went up like kindling."

"Where's our boarder?"

"The Chinaman?" He shrugged. "Don't know yet. You and your girl were lying out here when we arrived. We figure he must have gone back in for something and been trapped. But he'll turn up. Teeth don't burn."

I looked up at him. For the doctor, the sequence of events was obvious. The Chinaman had given his life for ours and had we been more valued citizens of Galen, what he did might have seemed heroic. Galen would think he perished in the fire. For Galen, there was no mystery in what had happened. For me, there was nothing but mystery, one that would endure into my old age. He'd had no reason to go back into the inn. We three were the only occupants. But his arrival in a town that offered him nothing had been similarly improbable. What had brought him?

Toward dawn, the inn finally burned itself out, leaving a charred staircase as the only evidence a home had once stood, a house wherein some people, who had never amounted to much, had lived and died, loved and cursed each other. My bedroom door, like most everything else, was burned to cinder, but its locks had not been destroyed. Even melted into a twist of metal, I could see where they had been pulverized, smashed to bits by some powerful force.

Another discovery awaited in the barn, where the fire had not reached. The body of Seth Hamilton. There was no blood or soot. He'd not been stabbed nor shot nor burned. His neck was simply broken, as neat as a chicken's meant for Sunday dinner.

In the days that followed, no one ever thought to pursue Seth's killer. Reverend's son or not, he'd long been more trouble than he was worth to Galen and with his mother and father and brother gone before him, there was no one to miss him in their lives or insist his death be avenged. Seth had outlived the few people who might have cared that he no longer walked the earth.

Nor did anyone think to find out for certain what had become of Chun Sung or Sung Chun; I never did find out which name went where. He was a foreigner, after all, and folks were satisfied that he'd perished with the inn, though no trace of him was ever found, not even the telltale teeth the doctor had predicted. But I knew. I felt certain that someday, in some dark corner of the world, I'd spy him disappearing down a twisting path, or glimpse him through the window of a passing train, his slanted eyes catching mine and holding for a moment, but only for a moment, before disappearing again. People always said Orientals were slippery, and now I had firsthand knowledge.

Rennie had her own theory about Mr. Sung. She thought the little man had not so much wandered to the inn as been invoked. By whom, I asked—for surely I'd not invited him. But she would only smile her dreamy smile that hinted at some secret communion and was not unlike the expression I had sometimes seen cross the features of our boarder. And I remembered their hushed conversations.

Not until some weeks later did I begin to understand, but only faintly, because whatever had transpired between them had not been for other eyes to see, and was not now for other minds to grasp. Rennie had summoned him and it was to Rennie alone that he had perhaps unveiled the mystery of himself.

We had been living in the barn because there was nowhere else to go, and mysteriously each day, a basket of food would appear, or a freshly baked loaf of bread, even once a mattress, as if Galen was afraid of its own timid compassion, a feeling that if allowed to grow might have led to further involvement and the further risk of sharing too closely in another's misfortune. And no one wanted that, least of all me. Sympathy would have only embarrassed me. So, they dropped food and snuck away as kindly and as stealthily as they had come.

I wondered if I could sell the blackened land where the inn had stood, and who in their right mind would buy it, and who, even if they were crazy enough to want to buy it, would have any money to buy it with. Conscience might make me confess that it was an unlucky place, cursed with old events, memories, personalities, convictions that do not burn but linger to haunt a house and the land it sat on for always, undimmed by time or the elements. In short, too much had happened there.

Then one day, not long after, while Rennie was at school, and I was sweeping the floor of the barn where Seth had got his neck broken, I sensed I wasn't alone, and looking up, I saw the silhouette of a man, illuminated from behind with the light of the morning sun. He seemed to have been standing there watching me for some time. Wordlessly, he came toward me, and with each step, his arms opened wider. And I went into those arms that had known me in hell, only to find me now in purgatory, and for the first time in years, I really looked at the sky, and I saw over his shoulder that there truly was something above the earth, a horizon that could not be sullied by it, that even tears could not obscure. And as I closed my eyes, my thoughts echoed the words he whispered into my hair. "I've come home," he said quietly. We held on to each other for a long time, then held each other far enough away to look at each other, only to clasp each other close again. And we probably would have gone on a long time like that—holding and looking and holding again, our eyes and arms so starved for the sight and feel of each other—had Rennie not come home from school.

She didn't seem particularly surprised to see him and when questioned, said she had always known he would come back for us. That that was simply the way it was to be.

Later when we were alone, Luca said that if Rennie had always known he'd come home, then she'd known more about it than he did, because his plan had been to go back to Italy when released and never to set foot on American shores again. He had been so angry at me for so long, been so convinced that I had wronged and betrayed him, felt so righteous about his indignation that he was sure he could not love me ever again. As for Rennie, he was convinced that she would be better off without a father who felt nothing but bitterness and resentment toward her mother. So his plan was to sail for Naples, find work, and send us money every month. It was hard to hear him talk about how much he had hated me, but I had to know. "What changed your mind?" I asked at last because so far, I had heard nothing that would make him want to come back for us.

Luca said a man had visited him in prison, the only visitor he had ever had except for my one visit to him. The man seemed to have known Rennie and me, though he never volunteered how he knew us. He spoke little and there was something peculiar about his speech, as if words were a foreign language that he had to translate from another medium. He told Luca that he would be released soon, and Luca didn't believe him because he still had almost a year to go on his sentence. He told him that he must go back to his wife and child and take them back to Italy with him where others would be waiting. Luca asked him why he *must* do this, and the man responded without a hint of sarcasm, "Otherwise the world will end."

Luca had laughed out loud at that and had begun to think it was a trick perpetrated by one of the other prisoners, who often tormented him because he was the warden's favorite. But the following week, he was told that he and a few other prisoners were being released unexpectedly to make room in the overcrowded prison for new offenders. Still Luca doubted on what authority the visitor had spoken with such conviction and he had not abandoned his own plan. He had gone so far as to enquire about the train schedule to New York and how much passage was to Naples. But very soon he realized that leaving us behind had only been what Rennie would call "for pretend."

In his anger, he had needed to pretend for awhile that it was possible to leave us. It wasn't. It had never been. We were a family for better or worse, not because he and I had uttered some words to each other fraudulently years ago, but because joy in each other and misery and longing had welded us together as surely as the flame-forged locks of my bedroom door. I realized, too, that in every moment that he had hated me, he had loved me in that very same moment, and that's the way of things that are joined and which "no man can put asunder."

I told Luca all about our boarder, how it must have been him who carried us out of the burning house, how he must have gone to visit Luca because everyone in the whole county knew where Luca was and why. And he said that all made sense, except that his visitor was tall and fair and not short and dark, and he looked more like a Viking than an Oriental. So we decided that it had been one of Galen's newsy bodies and left it at that. To continue to question it would just have caused an itch in our minds that could never be scratched.

I asked Luca how close Italy was to Kathmandu. He didn't know. I hadn't thought of Kathmandu for a long time. I felt certain that I would never in my life go there, and I didn't care. We imagine our zenith. But neither a zenith nor a nadir is fulsome enough to be the whole of a life, and ruined life is still life. I gave up Kathmandu for Naples, bartering a life that could never have been for one that was. An excellent trade, and there was no tragedy in it. It was as it should be. Or the world would end.

We booked passage to Naples a few days later, and when the time came for us to walk down our road for the last time, I turned to look at what was left of the inn and was surprised to feel nothing but relief that the past had been purged so completely. Jewel, my sisters, Aaron, Seth, I let them all go now, like birds I had held in my hand. *"And lo the bird is on the wing,"* Omar would have said.

When we stood on the deck of the ship pulling out of New York harbor, I looked at my child waving to people she did not know and my husband's profile as he gazed out at the receding land, and I felt what Eve must have felt on the first morning in the Garden. In the end, there was nothing left to do but sigh at the incoherent coherence of every life. Luca said the Italians had a saying: "*Since the house is on fire, let us warm ourselves.*" And we would.